"I came to ask you..."

"Ask me what?"

The same hesitation that had him trailing off gripped his features, his full lips slashing into a scowl and his face darkening more than the stormy gray clouds overtaking the skies.

"Ask me what, Alwan? If you haven't noticed, we're about to be rained on, and I'd really like for that not to happen—"

"Ask you to marry me."

Right as he spoke, thunder rumbled loudly over their heads, a warning of the downpour that would follow soon.

Wondering if she'd heard him correctly, Lulu stammered, "S-s-sorry? *Marry?*"

Alwan shut his car door and sealed the short space to her. Now close enough to touch, he filled her vision and commanded her full attention with that vehement gaze of his. So much so that she hadn't registered the drop of cold rainwater splashing onto her cheek. Not until Alwan reached out and swiped the wetness away with his thumb.

Then, shocking her anew, he said, "I want you to be my wife, Lulu."

Dear Reader,

I'll share a secret with you: writing has always been a bit therapeutic for me. And writing *Their Save-the-Date Charade* wasn't any different of an experience.

Throughout the story, Lulu and Alwan are constantly faced with certain things in their lives that are out of their control. But the one thing they *do* have power over is their fake engagement agreement. Of course, neither Lulu nor Alwan anticipates falling in love to complicate their relationship ruse!

Before they fall head over heels though, they do a lot of healing together. One big part of their emotional journey is learning to trust in letting go of the situations that are beyond their ability to control. (Admittedly something I struggle with at times!)

Because of this, it was tough writing some parts of their tale, but what made it all worth it was dreaming up the lighter, uplifting moments and looking forward to the promise of happiness and true love at the end.

I only hope that you feel the same!

Happy reading,

Hana x

THEIR SAVE-THE-DATE CHARADE

HANA SHEIK

Recycling programs for this product may not exist in your area.

ISBN-13: 978-1-335-47076-8

Their Save-the-Date Charade

For questions and comments about the quality of this book, please contact us at CustomerService@Harlequin.com.

Harlequin Enterprises ULC
22 Adelaide St. West, 41st Floor
Toronto, Ontario M5H 4E3, Canada
www.Harlequin.com

HarperCollins Publishers
Macken House, 39/40 Mayor Street Upper,
Dublin 1, D01 C9W8, Ireland
www.HarperCollins.com

Printed in U.S.A.

Hana Sheik falls in love every day reading her favorite romances and writing her own happily-ever-afters. She's worked various jobs—but never for very long because she's always wanted to be a romance author. Now she gets to happily live that dream. Born in Somalia, she moved to Ottawa, Canada, at a very young age and still resides there with her family.

Books by Hana Sheik

Harlequin Romance

The Abdullahis

Falling for Her Forbidden Bodyguard
Another Shot at Forever

Second Chance to Wear His Ring
Temptation in Istanbul
Forbidden Kisses with Her Millionaire Boss
The Baby Swap That Bound Them

Visit the Author Profile page at Harlequin.com.

To my hooyo and my big sister,

Two of the strongest women I know. Love you both!

CHAPTER ONE

"ALL RIGHT, WALK me through your logic again, just one more time." At the exasperated, sleep-roughened voice of his cousin, Alwan Eltahir tightened his hands on the steering wheel and snapped his narrowing eyes from the long, lonely stretch of country road ahead of him to the car's infotainment system.

Glaring at the glowing monitor as if his cousin Malek was right in front of him, he gritted out, "It's simple. I'm taking some time off to clear my head, and I can't do that right now in the city. So, if my parents call—"

"You mean *when* they do," Malek interjected with a long yawn. "Because they always do, Al. No one helicopter-parents like your mom and dad."

Alwan set his teeth but bit his tongue. There was no arguing that point.

"Fine. *When* they do, tell them I'm over at yours."

"So I'm your cover story. What's new?"

"I'm being serious. I don't need them calling me right now, so are you willing to help or not?"

"Give me a second," Malek told him, followed by the faint, muffled sound of voices and then rustling sheets, as though his cousin was rousing from bed, which made sense given the early hour.

While he waited for Malek, Alwan drummed his fingers over the steering wheel, impatience priming his every muscle. Malek finally yawned, "All right, I'm back. Rima says hello, by the way. She was wondering why this phone call of ours couldn't have waited another two or three hours."

Malek's wife, Rima, was a night-shift nurse.

Softly cursing, Alwan said, "Tell her I said I'm sorry for waking her. I wouldn't have called if I'd known she had the night off."

"Why *did* you call now? You know, besides wanting me to lie to Aami Omer and Khalti Ayaan for you?"

Hearing his parents' names reminded Alwan of everything that had led up to this very point, prompting a groan.

"This wouldn't have anything to do with what happened—"

"Don't. Just, please don't," Alwan cut Malek off, his cousin's chuckle destroying what little calm and peace of mind he had left. Like water through a crack in a dam, the memories first trickled warningly before spewing forth and sweeping him under.

It started a little more than two weeks ago—sixteen days to be precise, not that Alwan would ever admit to marking the hours and minutes, heck *each god-awful second*, as they sped by. No, on the outside he had held on to his usual cool facade, not giving away for a moment that he might not have everything under control.

That his world was possibly a breath away from implosion.

Oh, like that hasn't happened already...

The sarcastic thought had him wringing the steering wheel and pressing his foot down on the accelerator, pushing the small car's engine. Anyone would think he was running away from his problems, and, in a way, he already had. Fleeing everything and everyone he'd known in Toronto, Alwan skulked out of his condo and the city late last night without notifying his family…and the few friends who hadn't yet abandoned him after his so-called villainy was caught in 4K.

The video that had made him an internet villain had been uploaded and *re*-uploaded so many times that he couldn't close his eyes without clearly visualizing it. The seven-minute clip of his confrontation with an angry, now former, client who hadn't liked the way Alwan had handled his defense was branded into his brain. It had taken place in the busy coffee shop on the first floor of his law firm's office building, in the middle of the day, where naturally it had been caught on a phone camera.

Although Alwan could be seen having an assortment of pastries lobbed at him while his client loudly and indiscriminately aired his grievances, it apparently hadn't mattered that *he* had actually been the victim of the altercation.

The video went viral overnight and the internet had held court and swiftly deemed him as the aggressor. All because he was the fancy-schmancy lawyer. Meanwhile, his ex-client, a widower suburban dad of two who had "just been trying to make ends meet" and was "counting on the disputed family inheritance to support his children," had garnered the hearts and sympathies of the public.

It wasn't even the public's opinion he cared about. Alwan's problem was that his law firm had taken one look at the impact his negative image was having on them, and decided he was a liability. They hadn't exactly framed it like that, but how else was he supposed to interpret his bosses foisting a sudden paid leave on him and practically pushing him out the front door?

"It's not fair," Alwan grumbled.

"Yeah, well, it's already happened. No point in

sulking now. The question is, what are you going to do about it?" Malek pressed.

"I have a plan."

For a beat, the silence on Malek's end was punctuated by the distinct sounds of clinking tableware and whirring from a coffee machine. Then he sighed. "Okay, I'll bite. Does this plan happen to involve you getting married to please your parents?"

Alwan scowled immediately, flustered and annoyed. "They told you. When?"

"A couple days ago, and your parents didn't tell me. Mine did."

"Of course they did."

"Did you really think your mom and dad were going to keep it a secret? They've been trying to get you married off for *years*." His cousin chuckled.

Alwan figured his days at his firm were numbered, so he'd had to think outside the box. Starting his own practice had always felt like an out-of-reach dream, mainly because it required the kind of singular focus he didn't have around his high-demand work schedule. But now that he had been temporarily benched, the idea of being his own boss had firmly taken root and wouldn't budge.

That was where his parents and their bargain came in.

Because despite not wanting to accept their help, this time he saw no other option than to throw himself at their mercy in order to get access to their network of high-net-worth contacts.

"I get potential clients and they see me get married. We're all happy," Alwan said, sounding decidedly very *un*happy.

"You're doing this for clients?" Malek tsked. "Man, cuz, that's cold. Even a little sad. Have you considered what your future wife might think?"

"It will be mutually beneficial and she'll be free to leave the marriage…just as soon as my firm is up and running."

"Seems like you have it all worked out. I guess the big question that's left is why do you need me to cover for you?"

Because I feel like I'm going to have a breakdown at any moment, was what Alwan would have said if he hadn't cared about worrying his cousin. As annoying as Malek could be though, he didn't deserve the kind of burden that came with the fear churning away in Alwan's gut. Fear of what the future held in store for him, and fear that he couldn't escape his past mistakes.

Giving his head a shake, he cleared his suddenly hoarse throat.

"I just need to clear my head, that's it. A few days is all I'm asking. Hold them off that long, and I'll owe you one."

"Fine, I'll try to keep your parents from finding you. Speaking of, where are you anyways?"

"Alberta."

Malek's spit take was loud. "Alberta! What's in Alberta?"

Not what. *Who.*

Alwan had lied to his parents about having a fiancée the day before, and now he needed to make it true—and preferably before they discovered his deception.

But rather than divulge his problem to Malek and endure more questions and opinions, he quickly thanked his cousin and ended the call before setting his phone on silent.

Noticing that the sky was even brighter now, the warm golden rays of dawn peeking above the snowcapped mountains in the far horizon gave him an unexpected burst of hope that Alwan hadn't felt for a long time. Hope that he hadn't made a mistake in venturing so far away from home, and that everything—

Everything would be all right after all.

"Don't worry, Blue, everything's going to be fine." Lulu Sadiq wished she felt more confident as she looked from the inquisitive blue eyes of her cat up at the gathering storm clouds above the treetops.

When she and Blue had left for their early

morning hike, the sky had been clear and filled with brilliant sunlight, but now that pleasant mid-April weather was being chased away by brisk, bone-chilling winds.

A shiver rippled through her in spite of all the layers she wore.

Somehow Lulu didn't think that the weather could be entirely blamed. Since waking, she hadn't been able to shake a sense of impending dread.

At first she presumed it might be the worrying sounds coming from her RV lately. Sounds that predicted repair bills in her near future.

No, that's not why. She shivered again when a new wave of agitation ghosted over her.

Spring frost crunched under her hiking boots as she slowly resumed her trek down the path that would take her and Blue back to their warm, cozy four-wheel shelter. Lulu smiled down at her furry companion in his cat carrier. He had his wet pink nose and a paw pressed to the clear bubble window, like he was telling her to hurry up before the storm decided to unleash its wrath.

"Don't worry. We'll be home soon." She grinned when Blue meowed impatiently and pawed at the window, his way of telling her to leg it and quickly. "Okay, okay, I hear you. I'm moving." She hitched the cat carrier over her shoulders and set off at a steadier clip.

She huffed and puffed, the exertion taking away any lingering foreboding thoughts. Before long the shadowy tree line broke up ahead and she smiled to herself.

"We're home, Blue," she called back to her cat, not caring if another hiker caught her talking to her four-legged friend.

Smiling widely, Lulu crossed the wooden markers indicating the end of the footpath and walking trail—

And stopped in her tracks, her widening eyes flitting from the welcome sight of her RV to the small two-door car parked beside it.

She wasn't expecting any visitors.

In fact, avoiding the people in her life was why Lulu had been on the road for a year now. After her divorce it had been hard to pretend that she was doing all right. Harder because she hadn't shared with her family what had led to the end of her marriage.

Unconsciously, she slid her hand down from her chest to her lower belly.

Losing a baby wasn't an experience she'd wish on even the worst of her enemies.

It had felt like someone had reached in and ripped out a vital part of her and left a gaping hole in its place. And, in a way, that was exactly what had happened. On the outside she'd long healed, but inside there were these floating fragments, tiny shards that sliced at her when she so much as thought of everything that could've been and everything that wasn't meant to be.

Was *this* what she'd been feeling was coming for her?

Knowing that she wouldn't get answers standing there, she stiffened her upper lip and drew her shoulders down from where they were brushing her earlobes. She tightened her grip on the straps of her kitty carrier and reminded herself that she wasn't alone. Blueberry was with her, and her Birman cat was her fiercest protector. If anything, she should feel sorry for whoever had decided to come searching for her.

Marching toward the intruder in the small car, Lulu willed a courage she didn't entirely feel right then. She squinted at the darkly tinted car windows and barely made out that no one was behind the wheel. Perplexed, she ground to a halt beside the driver's window and looked around yet again.

The reserved sites of the RV park and campground were at the base of a double-peak mountain in the Canadian Rockies. But no one was driving a small car like the one in front of her. Around these parts, where the wilderness could sometimes deter a smaller vehicle from full exploration, it would've already stood out even if the owner hadn't chosen to invade her reserved spot. She wondered if it was a tourist who had come from the campground nearby. Someone who was new to the area and had accidentally made a mistake and encroached in her space.

A glance at the license plate revealed nothing except that the plate was Alberta-issued.

So, who, then? Tourist, local... Murderer.

Lulu gave her head a shake, the last possibility chilling her more than the winds that were gusting now. She'd been listening to too many true crime podcasts. Still, she couldn't see the harm in erring on the side of caution. Pulling out her phone from her coat pocket, Lulu muttered, "I'll just call the park authorities, then."

But something kept her from pressing their number in her contact list.

That same something had her tucking her phone away, leaning forward and cupping her hands around her squinched eyes to peer through the tinted car window.

Lulu yelped and launched back.

The driver was in the car after all.

Heart racing and mouth quickly drying, she scrambled back out of reach as the driver opened the car door. She watched, wide-eyed, as a man stepped out.

"Alwan!"

Lulu looked him up and down, from his short, curly black hair and handsome brown face to his stylish overcoat, casual dress shirt, slim fit trousers and shiny leather boots, her brain still struggling to reconcile that he was standing before her.

"The beard's new," she blurted before snapping her lips together in embarrassment.

Raising his brows, he lifted a hand and scrubbed his bearded cheek. "Not really. I've been growing it for a while now."

"Oh?" she said, "I guess it's just a testament to how long it's been since I've seen you."

He simply nodded and stared at her sharply.

So sharply it had Lulu shuffling awkwardly in place, gazing back at him like a deer transfixed by headlights. The apprehension she'd been carrying around since the morning crept over her again. Only this time it wasn't this amorphous fear floating around just out of reach. Right in that moment Lulu could affix her uneasiness to the way Alwan was staring at her with a hawkish glint to his eyes.

He was the last person she ever thought she'd see in this secluded part of Alberta.

As far back as Lulu could remember, she and Alwan had shared something of a rivalry.

Born the same year, their unspoken childhood friction could be blamed on their parents constantly comparing the two of them. Lulu had grown up having to listen to her father and mother *sing* Alwan's praises all while pointing out *her* flaws and mistakes. She knew the same thing had to be happening to Alwan to some degree because he always looked as miserable as she did at their families' friendly gatherings.

The way Alwan was looking at her in that very instant had her recalling all the sullen glares he'd cast her way back in the past.

Only this time he isn't really glaring...

Rather, his intense stare had her stomach churning anxiously, her chest squeezing with a confusingly unfamiliar sensation and her heart beating faster than it should. Not liking the feelings he'd engendered in her one bit, and taking the rolling sounds of thunder above as a sign, Lulu opened her mouth to get some answers. And maybe, hopefully, get Alwan away from her.

"What are you doing here?" she asked with a frown. "Did my parents send you? Ladna?"

"No, your parents and sister didn't."

Perplexed, Lulu racked her brain and snapped her fingers when she landed on an answer. "It was Liban, wasn't it?" Her younger brother had always looked up to Alwan, so much so that he followed in his career footsteps and was currently studying away from home at a highly ranked law school in Chicago. If anyone had sent Alwan to her, there was a strong likelihood the culprit was Liban.

Sure enough, Alwan nodded, explaining, "Yes

and no. Liban told me you were traveling someplace in Alberta last he spoke to you, but he didn't say where exactly. He *did* mention you posted on your socials regularly from the places you visited. From there it wasn't too hard to track you down."

Lulu blinked, a little astonished and unnerved that he'd gone to such lengths to find her. Whatever Alwan was after had to be important…and possibly dangerous to her. Even more wary now, she drawled, "Okay, Mr. Internet Sleuth, now you've found me, why are you here?"

"I came to ask you…"

Hesitation gripped his features, his full lips slashing into a scowl and his face darkening more than the stormy gray clouds overtaking the sky.

"Ask me what, Alwan? If you haven't noticed, we're about to be rained on, and I'd really like for that not to happen—"

"Ask you to marry me."

Right as he spoke, thunder rumbled loudly over their heads, a warning of the downpour that would follow shortly. Only now the threat of rain soaking them was so far from her mind. Pushed out instead by what Alwan had just said.

Wondering if she'd heard him correctly, Lulu stammered, "S-s-sorry? *Marry?*"

Alwan shut his car door and sealed the short space to her. Now close enough to touch, he filled her vision and commanded her full attention with that intense gaze of his. So much so that she hadn't registered the cold drop of rain splashing onto her cheek. Not until Alwan reached out and swiped the wetness away with his thumb.

Then, shocking her anew, he said, "I want you to be my wife, Lulu."

CHAPTER TWO

"LUULA, DID YOU hear me?"

Alwan's hand brushed her cheek again, his thumb caressing her, his touch so gentle it had her heart quivering. She heard him speak her full name, but the rest of what he said was coming down a long fuzzy tunnel at her, slowly drifting past the stupor immobilizing her limbs and rendering her speechless. The only thing that burst through was the irrationally strong urge to lean into the solid warmth of his palm—

He feels so nice... So safe.

Startled by that thought, Lulu quickly pushed his hand away and reared back.

Just like that, whatever spell he cast over her was broken.

"Wh-what are you d-doing?" She almost groaned aloud at her stammering. Revealing that he'd affected her was the last thing she wished to do, particularly when it felt like he had the upper hand right then.

"You had a raindrop, right there." He pointed

a finger at her face, those dark eyes of his vigilant in a way that had her body heating up and not so unpleasantly. "It was distracting."

"You know that's not what I mean. You *proposed* to me just now!"

Alwan's brows snapped up and, frowning, he clarified, "I wasn't proposing a *real* marriage. Just a fake engagement."

Her eyes bugged out at him. "Sorry? And how is that any better?"

He winced, though she wasn't sure if it was because of her shrill tone or whether he was finally cluing in to how appalling his words really were.

"Can I at least explain myself? I promise I'm not losing my mind," he said, his tone as even-keeled and serious as his now grave expression.

It was almost as worrying as how comfortable she'd felt being touched by him.

The rain pelting down a little harder and faster, Lulu flipped her coat hood over her head, wrapped her arms around herself and narrowed her eyes. Sure, he looked *and* sounded sincere...but she was still reluctant to believe that this wasn't all some elaborate, twisted joke. Of course, she then had to wonder—

Who is he trying to fool, and why?

They barely knew each other and, at least in the past, barely cared to get to know one another. Why marriage of all things, and why her? Because although they didn't know each other all too well, Alwan had to have known about her divorce, making what he'd just asked of her cruel.

Lulu bit the inside of her cheek, trying to ignore the way her eyes suddenly smarted. She told herself it wasn't tears blurring her vision, rather the rain coming down in sheets now and shrouding the world in a gray mist.

I should turn around, ignore him and walk away.

Meowing from inside his carrier over her back, Blue certainly thought they should take cover from the heavy rainfall and rumbling thunder.

But instead she stayed rooted to her spot and demanded, "I need you to explain yourself."

"Sure, okay." His tweed overcoat was now darker around his shoulders, his hair curling more from the extra moisture, and he blinked fast to keep rainwater from his eyes. "But can I do the explaining inside my car or your motor home?"

No sooner had he asked then a bolt of lightning briefly illuminated the churning sky. Unsurprisingly, this lightshow was then followed by a loud crack of thunder. Only now the thunder sounded ominously close to where they were standing.

"Fine," she agreed, backing toward her RV and giving his cramped-looking car the briefest of glances. "But I'd prefer my motor home."

"Let me just grab my things."

"Things?" Lulu began to ask, but he moved toward the back of his car and pulled a black travel bag from his trunk.

Locking up his car, Alwan hauled the duffel over his head as a makeshift umbrella.

Lulu unlocked the door to her RV and impatiently waved him in.

Ignoring the inexplicable heat blazing through her as he brushed past her, Lulu closed the door and turned to find Alwan surveying her home.

He was completely oblivious to her rising ire until she sharply cleared her throat.

Of course, now that she had his complete attention, his stare was just as intense and unreadable as ever. Unbidden, her stomach did a little shimmy on her. And it wasn't the only body part acting up. Her heart thumped a little louder in her ears and her urge to fidget was only growing the longer his eyes bore into her.

She gulped quietly. She needed to get ahold of the situation.

"Okay, let's get some rules down first." Rules would keep them on the same level of understanding.

Alwan nodded. "It's your home."

"Good. Shoes off, then," she remarked dryly, watching him glance down at the puddle forming on the vinyl flooring under his dressy boots.

He stepped forward, drawing to a halt when Lulu kissed her teeth.

Slowly, while maintaining eye contact, Alwan slipped off his boots.

Satisfied that he wouldn't track the mess all over her motor home now, she gestured at him. "You're dripping everywhere."

"You want me to take my clothes off too?"

"I didn't say that," Lulu snapped, cheeks flushed warm as she shuffled from foot to foot.

His lips twitched in a clear effort to hold back his humor, but wisely he just gave a nod and stood there silently awaiting her next instruction.

"My second rule is that you dry off. The bathroom is over there." She pointed behind him to a sliding door. "I'll just grab you a towel."

Once he was ensconced in the bathroom she blew a sigh. Inviting him inside her home might not have been her brightest idea, but she couldn't exactly toss him out now either. Not when rain hammered the roof and sides of the RV.

Freeing Blue from his carrier, he immediately crept over to sniff around the trail of water and Alwan's boots.

"We have a guest," she told him when he looked up and meowed at her for answers.

Not seeming to like that response, he high-tailed it to the bedroom.

Lulu sighed again, wishing she could hide too,

and wait out the storm and Alwan's temporary stay from the solitary safety of her bed. Instead of giving in to that thought, she rooted around her small linen cupboard for that towel she'd promised him.

Once she found it, Lulu rapped lightly on the bathroom door, called, "Hey, the towel's on the floor outside the door," and started crouching to set the towel down.

When she'd installed the barn door on the bathroom, she never once thought that she would come to regret it even slightly. But that was only because she hadn't ever imagined Alwan would be there with her. That he would slide open the door so fast and catch her mid-crouch, her face level with his lower half. Thankfully for her, he was still dressed in his wet clothes.

But being up close now, Lulu noticed how tightly his soaked trousers clung to his lean legs and his wet shirt suctioned to his abs and pecs and—

Snapping upright, towel still grasped in her hands, she gawped at him.

Knowing that she should look away, that she shouldn't be fixated on the water pooling at the base of his throat or be curious about the droplets trailing down past the open collar of his button-down shirt, Lulu gulped hard.

"Thanks." Alwan reached for the towel.

Loosening her grip, she held it out slowly. Their fingers brushed and she instantly recalled the feel of his long, thick fingers swiping at her cheek and his warm palm framing her face, making her feel secure, protected. All at once the flutters from her stomach swept up into her rib cage, whipped against her racing heart and raged into a windstorm when he huskily said her name.

"Luula? Anything else?"

"Just the third rule," she gritted, annoyed at her reaction to him and grasping for an excuse as to why she was still standing there. "Don't mess up my bathroom."

"Noted," he said and gave her a final piercing look before sliding the door close between them.

A heartbeat later the shower switched on, and her mouth dried at the image of him standing under the new high-pressure showerhead she'd installed, luxuriating in it the way she did regularly. Only now whenever Lulu used her shower, she would always remember Alwan and this moment.

Stop it. Stop thinking about him like this.

Confused by the way he had her feeling, Lulu compelled her stiff limbs to move away. Her eyes landed on the puddle around his boots and the tracks he'd made from her front entrance. She rolled up her sleeves and fetched her mop, suddenly all too glad for the chore.

Once she'd finished cleaning, she started a pot of coffee and hurried past the bathroom and into her bedroom. Drawing the ceiling-mounted privacy curtain closed, she rushed through changing into dry clothes, all the while keeping an ear open to any sounds of Alwan having finished with his shower.

From his resting place in the center of the bed, Blue gave her another of his mystified looks.

Her face was still a little hot when Alwan finally joined her.

"Coffee," he said with a smile, perking up instantly the way she often did at the promise of caffeine. "You shouldn't have."

"Well, I haven't had breakfast yet, and I thought it would have been rude if I didn't offer a cup to my *guest*." She stressed the last part on purpose, eyeing the duffel he'd carried over to the dinette as he pulled out one of the two chairs at the table.

Sitting, Alwan followed her gaze to the travel bag at his feet.

"It's as if you planned a longer stay," she said suspiciously. "Were you just *that* confident that I would agree to your bizarre idea of us getting engaged?"

He smiled, full lips slowly tugging up at the corners, his eyes squinting and his husky chuckle rolling through her not unlike the thunder rumbling outside the motor home.

"Don't worry. Once the storm clears, I'll leave," he reassured her, reaching for the mug she'd set down on the table between them. "And speaking of shelter, I appreciate you offering a place."

Returning his smile, Lulu hovered her hand over his cup at the last moment and bit the inside of her cheek when he scowled and looked between her and the coffee she was withholding. "Not so fast. You can thank me with an explanation."

He owed her that much after his bombshell proposal.

Though as much as she wanted answers, it didn't bode well that Alwan sighed and scrubbed at his bearded jaw.

"Okay, then." Heaving another long breath, he settled his palms on the table and leaned back in his chair. "Where do I start?" he said before launching into his explanation.

"That's a lot," Lulu said once he finished rehashing the tale of his professional downfall. Taking pity on him, she moved away the hand blocking his access to the coffee mug and even smiled when he took his first sip and sighed with a blissful look on his handsome face.

"I'm just surprised you hadn't heard about it already, or even seen the video."

"I've been living a little off-grid, if you haven't noticed." She waved at their setting before sobering up. "I am sorry that happened to you. It doesn't seem very fair."

"It isn't," he echoed, his hands squeezing the heated ceramic cup in his grasp as angry helplessness furrowed his brow and twisted his mouth into a scowl. "It didn't matter that my client cooled down eventually, gave me a sincere apology and requested that I appeal his case. Because by that point the video had millions of views, and my firm was being targeted by online trolls.

"Naturally my bosses asked me to drop the appeal and let my client go quietly."

"But you didn't drop it," Lulu said, having connected the dots herself.

He shook his head. "I couldn't. And when they found out, they benched me. It's reinforced for me that I should be running my own legal practice. Helping whomever I want to help without having anyone looking over my shoulder. Sadly though, I'm not entirely in a position to do that at the moment. I need influence and wealth from the kind of high-net-worth clients that have both.

"On top of that, with everything that's happened online, my image isn't very polished right now and clients might not trust me."

"And getting engaged would help fix your professional reputation, is that it?"

"Not exactly, but some of the wealthy clients I'm targeting are older, therefore more traditional-minded. To them, marriage equals respectability. Besides, having a fiancée would also ease my parents' worries for me. *Hopefully...*"

She recognized that look on his face from having stared at her own reflection in the past, when she'd felt helpless in her own body. Useless and out of control...

Powerless to stop her baby from dying.

Lulu squeezed her eyes closed, breathed slowly and methodically through her nose before opening her eyes just as the lights flickered.

Thankfully Alwan hadn't noticed her reaction. Preoccupied with the electrical hiccup that lasted a few short flickers, he had his head raised to the pendant light above the dinette.

"Uh, should we be concerned? I didn't exactly pack a flashlight."

"The lights do that sometimes, especially during bad weather like this. I already unplugged from the shore power and lowered the antenna, so there's no risk of the storm frying the electrical system," she assured him, not certain it was working since he grimaced at the thunder cracking noisily outside.

"So that means no chance of *us* getting fried either, right?" he hedged.

"I promise I won't let you get electrocuted… At least not until you've answered all my questions." She smirked when he gave her another of his pleasant-sounding chuckles. Just like that the anxiety that had reared out of nowhere was gone as quickly as it had manifested. Lulu couldn't shake the feeling that Alwan had helped with that somehow, even if it felt like all he'd done since he'd shown up out of the blue was throw her off-kilter, annoy her and ruin her morning.

Although right now he seemed to be cooperative, even asking, "What do you want to know next?" as if he didn't mind being interrogated.

Not that this is an interrogation.

Since he offered though, Lulu wondered, "I understand why you feel you have to get engaged for your career, but surely you could propose to any other woman?" She blushed with him gazing intently at her again. "Why me?"

What does any of this have to do with me?

It was the question she'd wanted to ask all along.

Before Alwan could answer her, the lights winked again. Once, twice. And then they were gone altogether, plunging them into darkness.

* * *

"Nope. The lights are still out," Alwan called out to Lulu after pulling open the door to her RV and taking a peek into the darkness inside.

The electricity to her motor home had gone out half an hour ago, and once the rain had slowed and the thunder seemed to have rolled past them, Lulu insisted on taking a look at the generator. Even though Alwan hadn't wanted to venture out into the wet, chilly world outside, he also couldn't in good conscience lounge around while she attempted to restore their lost power.

But since he didn't know the first thing about RV maintenance, all he ended up doing was holding a flashlight steady for her to work the circuit breakers. That and occasionally jogging back to check whether any of the lights had come back on.

This was the third time he'd investigated with no change in their lightless situation.

It was also when the rain picked up again and Lulu threw up her hands and called, "I give up."

Already warmer and dryer, Alwan was all too happy to be indoors again. But when Lulu set up a couple more camping lights to cast off the dark, his spirits dampened the second he saw her frown illuminated by the lantern she set down on the table.

Concerned, he asked, "What's wrong?"

"It's nothing." If she was trying to sound convincing, she failed the instant she sighed softly. Barely sparing him a glance, Lulu sat back at the table and, grabbing her mug, took a big gulp of her coffee.

Following her lead, he sat too and gave her a pressing look. "It doesn't sound like nothing."

Lulu lowered her cup slowly.

"Do you want to talk about whatever it is? I'm a good listener, or so I've been told."

"Oh, are you?" She smiled suddenly and it tripped his alarms.

"It kind of comes with my profession."

"I bet it does," she said with a breezy laugh.

Those alarms were now blaring for him to zip his lips, but even if he had, it was too late.

Lulu's smile disappeared in a blink.

"Strange," she said. "You're a good listener, but you still haven't managed to listen and answer my question. Why propose to me?"

Alwan clenched his jaw. It wasn't Lulu's fault for being curious. In fact, he'd anticipated she would have questions. Any normal person would.

She wants answers. Give them to her.

At least this way he possibly stood a chance at turning her around on the admittedly outlandish idea of her playing his fake fiancée.

"I told you my parents want to see me married, and I need their connections to gain new clients and eventually, that is hopefully sooner rather than later, open my private practice. It's our quid pro quo agreement. Doesn't that explain everything?"

She rolled her eyes. "Everything *but* why you chose me. Like I said, I'm sure you have plenty of options available to you."

"Is that a compliment on my good looks?"

He braced himself for a tongue-lashing. As young children forced to grow up in each other's company, she'd often made a point of calling out his ego. Just as he'd rarely passed up a chance at riling her up. And when they hadn't been taking passive-aggressive digs at each other, Lulu avoided Alwan and he steered clear of her.

Now Alwan sought her out purposefully. *Because I need her.*

It was unlike him to depend on others—to *trust* them. He didn't give his confidence away easily. After all, trusting the wrong people was what created this mess for him in the first place.

Trusting his bosses to have his back no matter what, considering all the years he'd toiled away like a model soldier ant on behalf of the firm.

Then he'd trusted his parents to support him no strings attached, but they had bargained with him instead…almost as if they didn't trust *him*.

Why would they after what happened with Hashim?

He froze, muscles tensing at that thought.

It wasn't often that Alwan allowed his mind to drift to his older brother. At least not anymore, not after he had taught himself to repress any recollections of him. And now was the last place he wanted that bleak stroll down memory lane.

He was grateful then when Lulu murmured, "You're incorrigible."

Instead of biting his head off, she turned her head away and gave him a different view of her beauty.

Shoulder-length, wavy black hair framing a heart-shaped face, beautiful russet red-brown skin, deep soulful-brown eyes ringed by naturally long black lashes and those lushly full lips of hers had him a little weak at the knees.

"I heard about your plan to return home soon."

Eyes saucer-wide, Lulu snapped her head back to him, any signs of her adorable bashfulness gone.

He couldn't explain it, but it felt like the rest of the world blinked out of existence, the darkness sucking everything else away and leaving just him and Lulu. Gazing into her eyes, losing himself in the depth of her stare, he dragged a tongue over his dry lips and breathed through the anxiety pressing down over his chest. "That's why I *need* you."

"Alwan…"

Steeling himself against the tantalizing shiver the sound of his name in her soft, breathy voice elicited, Alwan pressed his palms closer together, his short nails digging into the backs of his hands. Like a punch to the gut, desire for her caught him unawares, the heat of it more potent than anything he'd experienced before.

But he wouldn't let it control this moment. Couldn't trust it not to ruin his careful planning.

"You need me?" Lulu repeated quietly.

Plucking open his collar did little to cool the fire in his blood, but at least he managed to untangle his tongue and said, "I… I meant that I require your help."

"Oh" was all she said in turn. And was it his imagination, or did she sound disappointed?

Not wanting to analyze that any closer, Alwan moved on. "There's a reason why I chose you. It's because unlike other women I've met, I know you won't complicate any of this with emotion."

"Why do you think that?"

"Your divorce."

Any hint that she might desire him too disappeared in a flash. Lulu's face grew stony, her eyes two chips of ice freezing him where he sat.

"What about my divorce?"

He wasn't deceived by the calm she portrayed. "The women I've met expect marriage, but they also want love. And it's only made me realize that love… Love isn't something I desire."

"You think because I'm divorced, I wouldn't want love either," she said, an arctic chill creeping into her voice.

"No. That's not—" He cut himself off, took a breath and recognized that he had one shot at not bungling this and losing her completely. Taking a moment, he gathered his courage. "What I'm trying to say, without sticking my foot in my mouth, is that I think that you'd understand what this could be and not confuse it with anything else."

"And what could it be?"

"A partnership," Alwan said confidently.

"Partners. Us?"

"Yes. And we'd both benefit. For instance, I'd be more than willing to negotiate reimbursement."

"You'd *pay* me to be your bride?"

"My *fake fiancée*, yes."

Lulu pressed her lips together and, still looking wary, she finally asked, "How much are we talking?"

Alwan fought back the urge to triumphantly pump his fist. "Does that mean you're interested?"

"It means that I'm questioning my sanity for even thinking about it." Closing her eyes, she rubbed her temple with two fingers. After a little while she fixed him with a glare. “Let’s be clear though, I haven’t agreed to anything. Not yet.”

This time he couldn’t contain his excitement. Grinning, he said, “So, not a complete ‘no,’ and just not yet a ‘yes.’ That’s still promising.”

“Don’t push it,” she cautioned with a frown.

Alwan laughed. “Fine. But can I suggest a better location while you do your thinking? I could book us a hotel. A really nice one.”

“You’re trying to bribe me.”

“Is it working?”

Lulu flung up her hands and huffed her exasperation. “Like I said, incorrigible. You know what? Do whatever you want, Alwan. I have to feed my cat.” As annoyed as she sounded, Alwan could’ve sworn her lips switched up into a smile as she stood. It was hard to tell with it being so dark, and even harder when she breezed away without a look backward. But he took it as a promising sign.

One, he hoped, that would fix all his problems.

CHAPTER THREE

ALWAN COULDN'T HELP the spring in his step as he led Lulu into their luxury hotel suite. He had good cause to be happy. The first phase of overturning his recent bad luck was well underway now, and it was starting to look like he hadn't clung on to hope for nothing.

Eyes wide and mouth open, Lulu trailed slowly after him. Almost as though she was afraid she'd break one of the many fragile vases or ornate chandeliers they passed in the castle-like, historic grand railway hotel.

Alwan hid his smile when he heard her soft gasp as they strolled past the rooms, the long winding hallway with its highly polished dark hardwood flooring ending in a grand living room. The room's primary feature was the panoramic view: the surrounding forest, the snowcapped mountains this area of Alberta was known for, and the nearby sweeping green valleys.

Like she was drawn in by a magnet, Lulu drifted to one of the tall, wide windows.

"What do you think?" Alwan asked, coming up behind her.

Startling, Lulu half turned to him and pressed a hand to her chest.

"Are you trying to give me a heart attack? Need I remind you that you might want me alive and well for this plan of yours."

Laughter bubbled out of him like fizz out of a shaken soda bottle. It was instantaneous and seemingly infectious by the way Lulu sucked in her lips and looked away quickly, almost like she was not only holding in her laugh but hiding it from him too.

"I'll take your distraction as a sign that you approve of the hotel," Alwan practically purred, a little too pleased with himself.

With a little huff, she fully turned away and folded her arms, forcing him to step up beside her and gaze down at her instead.

"But if you don't like it, we can always see about an upgrade."

"An upgrade?" Lulu looked around them, surveying the whole room before her eyes landed squarely back on him. "To what exactly? This place is already bonkers-level luxurious." Under her breath she muttered, "Are you going to buy the whole castle next?"

Alwan threw back his head and laughed.

"I would if I could, especially if I knew it

would win you over on my plan," he said, wiping the tears of laughter from his eyes and chuckling again.

She sniffed and punched her nose up into the air. "Well, maybe I'm not a castle kind of girl."

"Then *maybe* you need to be convinced." As he spoke, Alwan pulled in closer, amused when her nonchalant facade broke and she sharply turned her head from him. He would've teased her more had her cat not chosen that moment to interrupt, meowing incessantly from its carrier.

Lulu unzipped the bag and pulled the little furry beast out into the open. Instantly locking those luminescent blue eyes on Alwan, her cat hissed at him.

"He doesn't seem to like me."

"Blue's a good judge of people."

Alwan shook his head at her barb, laughing again. "Are you sure you and the cat don't want separate suites?"

"And be more indebted to you? No thanks. Besides, there's plenty of room for all of us, and our bedrooms are on opposite ends of this massive suite."

"Touché," he said with a grin.

"Now if you don't mind, Blue and I are going to explore the rest of this place." Not waiting for a response, she flitted off.

He had every mind to pursue, especially with

the way her sweet, floral-scented perfume lingered in the air like a lure he knew would lead right to her. But not knowing what he would do or say when he caught up to Lulu held him back. Clenching his fists, he stared after her until she was out of sight and only then did he breathe slowly out through his nose, the tension gripping his muscles not fully expelled with the breath.

And it was because he'd felt his phone vibrate in his inner jacket pocket again.

The missed calls—seven in total—were all from his mom and dad.

There were also a few texts from his cousin explaining that Alwan's parents had already tried calling Malek to check on him, and Malek had convinced them that Alwan was currently crashing on his couch.

After sending his cousin a quick grateful text, he sighed wearily.

Alwan knew that this brief peace wouldn't last, and that his parents would show up on Malek's doorstep eventually if they didn't hear from him. And when they didn't find him there, they would send out search parties.

Closing his eyes, Alwan could just imagine what their faces would look like once he confessed that he had no prospective bride. That he had only lied because he'd had his back to a wall and it seemed the easiest thing to do at the time.

Instead, it was looking like all he'd ended up doing was delaying their inevitable disappointment with him.

Unless...

Unless Lulu helped him.

Alwan looked toward the empty corridor in the direction she'd gone, a curious longing to go to her stirring in his breast. The sensation, new and disconcerting, was not like anything he'd ever felt before.

It was nearly as worrying as the possibility that Lulu wouldn't agree to his fake engagement.

"Either you're having trouble deciding on what lunch will be, or something's bothering you."

Alwan's deep voice carried over to her from across the table they shared. Lulu shook her head, lowered the menu and met his inquisitive gaze.

"Does your distraction have anything to do with a repair quote for your RV that hasn't come in yet?"

She bit her lip, masking her surprise that he'd clocked her concern. Was she that easy to read, or was her stress over her nearly depleted bank account and the possibly exorbitant cost to fix her motor home just that obvious? After the storm had cleared up a few hours ago, they'd dropped the RV off at a repair shop on their way to the hotel and ever since then Lulu had been worrying nonstop.

Seeming to take her silence as an affirmative, Alwan moved on and asked, "Is that why you were preparing to wrap up your travels?"

"Yes…and no," she said, knowing the RV wasn't the only reason she was heading home.

After not having seen them for a year—the longest she'd gone without having any of them for company—Lulu missed her family greatly, and she knew they were worried about her still. So, it seemed a perfect time to let them see that she was doing all right. Show them that she'd long since recovered from the shock of her sudden divorce. And even though she wasn't ready to share her pregnancy loss with them, hopefully she could still give them some peace of mind.

At least that *had* been her plan before Alwan showed up with his outrageous proposal for them to pretend to be engaged.

Outrageous, but you're still considering it, aren't you?

Lulu curled her fingers tighter around the menu, the plastic covering creasing under the press of her fingernails.

If Alwan noticed the rising tension in her, he didn't show it when he asked, "By the looks of it, your motor home seems like an older model.

When you purchased it, did you consider you might need to repair it more?"

She glared at him for his insinuation that she hadn't properly planned for contingencies. "I *had* set appropriate funds aside for such an emergency, but I've also been renovating. Some of those costs may have gone beyond my budget."

"Then why not just ask your parents for the money?"

"I can't do that," she said sharply, her temper flaring up. "They have their shop to worry about, and our economy of late hasn't exactly been kind to small businesses. Not everyone is as lucky as your parents."

As soon as the words were out of her mouth, Lulu wanted to swallow them back. Alwan's parents had always been nothing but kind and generous to her and her family. They'd never treated her any different than their sons.

She stumbled through an apology.

"You don't have to apologize. Not when it's true that my parents are blessed with a successful business. I forget that not everyone has the same fortune." Alwan paused before wondering, "Are your parents not doing okay?"

"They're fine." She sighed. "I didn't mean to imply that their business is doing bad or anything, it's just I know the hard work they've put into the convenience store. I couldn't bother them with something as trivial as repairs on my motor home."

"Is it trivial though?"

Not knowing how to answer him, Lulu lowered her eyes back to her menu. She wasn't shocked by the expensive prices attached to the many different options of French Canadian cuisine, having gotten a clue of what the price range would be the instant she had set foot into the moody but elegant dining establishment.

Everything, including the exposed brick walls softened by gleaming dark wood accents in the tables, the vaulted ceiling's wooden beams, and the restaurant's golden lighting from drum chandeliers and wall sconces, added a warmth to the hushed, darkly intimate setting. It was the kind of restaurant that oozed fine dining.

"I think I'll butcher half these dishes names if I try to pronounce them. Also, is there nothing on here that's sensibly priced?"

Alwan's husky laughter had a sultry edge to it. "Can't say I'll be of much help with the French pronunciation, but lunch will be charged to the suite."

"You'll be paying for me. Again." Lulu compressed her lips, still unsure of how she felt about that. He'd been paying for everything. Their luxurious suite, the hotel's pet-sitting service to mind Blue while they were lunching, and now lunch itself. Knowing that he could likely afford it and then some didn't ease her troubled thoughts.

She knew what Alwan was up to. Softening her up with his lavish gifts was just a way to get her to sign on to his fake engagement ruse. But she hadn't made up her mind on whether she would just yet. And she didn't want him getting the wrong idea before she fully decided on what to do.

After they ordered she squared her shoulders and faced him. "Just so we're clear, I don't want you thinking that I've made a decision because you've been paying for everything. And I plan to pay you back for all of it, eventually."

"I know. Anything I can do to help you make up your mind?"

"Not really, though I do have a question."

"Ask away," he prompted.

"You know why I'm even entertaining this bizarre idea of yours, but I still don't understand why you have to go through all this? I can't imagine why your parents wouldn't just help you. Why the condition that you have to be engaged?"

"Besides wanting grandchildren." He rubbed his bearded jaw thoughtfully and smiled, only she sensed it was more forced than before. And she understood why when he said, "The only other reason I can fathom is they're worried about me."

"Because of that viral video?"

He gave her another tense smile. “Yes, there’s that, but I get the feeling they think I’m lonely. And that they believe by getting me married, that I’ll have someone by my side.”

“You’re clearly not happy about it though. Why not just tell them that?”

“Simple. I don’t want to disappoint them. You should’ve seen the way their eyes lit up when I told them I had a fiancée. They haven’t been that happy in a long while, and it feels cruel to snatch it away from them.”

She swallowed around the lump in her throat, relating more to what he’d said than she’d anticipated.

“Does that answer your question?” he asked.

Lulu nodded slowly. “I… I actually think I understand what you mean. After my divorce, I found the hardest thing to do wasn’t filing papers and packing my things and moving out of the home I shared with my ex. It was telling my parents, my family that my marriage had ended.

“All I could think about was having to face their disappointment when I’d moved back in with them.”

“And were they disappointed?” he asked, his attention completely riveted on her.

So much that he didn’t acknowledge the waiter who set down plates of amuse-bouches on their table. After filling their glasses with water, the waiter made himself scarce and, swallowing thickly, Lulu continued.

"They weren't. It was actually the opposite—they were just really concerned. I didn't mind it at first. But then, it got hard to be around them. No matter what I said, they worried about me. And it wasn't just my mom and dad, but my brother and sister too."

"Seems to be a shared trait of families. At least loving ones."

"Yeah, I suppose," she said softly and cast her eyes down at the artfully plated appetizer in front of them. "It's just, I couldn't take it anymore..."

"That's why you've been traveling for the past year."

She raised her head. "Is that what you're doing too?"

"Which do you mean, hiding or running? Because it feels like I'm doing both right now."

"So, what happens if I don't agree to your proposal?" she asked. "Will you run and hide forever?"

"I could ask the same of you. What will you do if you don't have enough funds for your repairs? Will you go back home and stay there, maybe pick up where you left off a year ago?"

"I don't know. At least not yet. But I know what you're still trying to do."

"And what is it that I'm *still* doing exactly?"

"You want me to agree, but as I've told you I haven't decided what I'll do."

He popped a small bite of flaky pastry in his mouth and chewed slowly and thoughtfully, swallowing before speaking. "I'd be lying if I said I didn't want your agreement. But I'd rather you do it of your own volition. Fake bride or not, your consent is the only nonnegotiable factor here."

Rendered speechless for a moment, Lulu watched him slice and spear a couple more bites of his profiterole. He ate neatly, all except for a small, mesmerizing spot of creamy goat cheese at the corner of his mouth. Though he wiped it away, she kept staring at where it had been, her own mouth going dry.

She knew she should stop, and that any second he would realize that she was looking at him weirdly, but she couldn't.

At least not until he caught her.

Alwan lifted a thick, black brow and an amused sparkle glimmered in his eyes.

Feeling her face heat up, Lulu bowed her head, mumbled, "Well, thank you, I guess," and picked up her knife and fork to try her own appetizer.

They lapsed into silence after that. And only once their plates were cleared and replaced with their entrées did Alwan speak up.

"So, how do you plan to spend the rest of your day?"

It reminded her that they were sharing a room. Even though the suite was expansive, far bigger than any hotel room she'd ever been in, Lulu knew it would still be hard to be near Alwan. Her body warmed all over at the mere thought of spending time in close quarters with him.

A part of her was regretting not taking Alwan up on his offer of a second suite.

"I'll probably go for a hike now that the weather is better," she said. "Take in the local sights and, um, clear my head."

"I'm guessing you don't want company?"

She shook her head and he smiled, his eyes crinkling with his genuine humor.

"What about you?" she asked quietly, her hand wrapping around her glass of ice water.

"Worried I'll be bored without you?"

And just like that, the tension was broken. Lulu scowled, the prick of guilt she was feeling about not offering him to join her on her hike evaporating into a puff of smoke.

"Not really. I'm sure your ego will keep you busy."

Alwan's low laugh was husky, the sound of it revitalizing her blushing cheeks, raising goose-flesh over her arms and unspooling an illicit heat in her lower belly.

It made her want to skip their meal altogether

and fast forward to the part where they went their separate ways for a little while.

Restraint didn't come easily to Alwan, but he had mastered it.

And yet all his practice in patience escaped him when Lulu left for her hike after their lunch together. He might have been all right with it had she not looked relieved when they parted ways. *Like she couldn't wait to be rid of me.*

In fairness, she'd asked for the time alone to think over the fake engagement, and not wanting to force her into agreeing, Alwan had let her go.

The first hour had been a brutal test in self-control. He'd paced like a caged animal in their hotel suite, hovering near the entrance.

When his legs finally tired of that, he briefly entertained the idea of heading out and trying to find her.

But one look out the window, at the immense sweeping landscape of forest, and he knew finding Lulu wouldn't be easy.

Once he put that idea to rest, he'd grabbed his tablet from his duffel bag and stalked out of their suite to find somewhere to work.

That was two hours ago.

Now he opened the door to their suite and walked in, tablet tucked under his arm, key card in his hand. At first nothing but the faint hum of the central heating greeted him. *She's still not back...* That realization tightened his muscles and had his thoughts racing to worrying scenarios, all of them centered around Lulu being injured.

What if she's hurt and can't get help?

Panic, hot and bilious, scorched up his throat.

Placing his tablet down on the entryway table, Alwan tightened his hand around the key card and was about to turn for the door and head to Reception to see if they could help when a flash of snow-white popped up in his peripheral.

Lulu's cat stared back at him from around the corner of the hall.

As soon as Alwan made eye contact, the furry beast gave a warning growl and shot off deeper into the hotel suite. Realizing that Lulu wouldn't have left her cat alone, as per the hotel's rules on pets, he understood it could only mean one thing. *She's here.*

Stuffing down the odd excitement surging up through him, he followed the direction her cat had gone.

It led him to the living-slash-dining room.

Striding in, he stopped short, a few things popping out at him immediately.

First, it was raining heavily again. Wind-driven rain splattered the windows, the sky full of dark, dense gray clouds now when it had been clear blue not too long ago. Second, the only other light source besides the pale natural light coming through the windows was the fiery glow of the electric fireplace. Finally, Lulu herself.

Curled up under a throw on the chaise lounge, and with a mug in her hands, she stared into the flames, either oblivious to him gazing at her or uncaring of his presence.

He had his answer when she said, “Are you just going to stand there and stare at me?”

“When did you get back?”

“Half an hour ago, just before it started pouring outside.” She turned her head to him then, the glow of the firelight casting off her lustrous dark hair and reflecting in her eyes as she looked him over. “Where were you?”

“Down at the bar, drinking my weight in drip coffee and working.”

Lulu hummed noncommittally before looking back at the fireplace.

“What about you? How was your trek into the great outdoors?”

“Okay” was her only response, and he got the distinct impression she was preoccupied.

He walked toward her, his glance flicking over to where her cat lounged on the armchair directly opposite where Lulu sat. The little beast growled low when Alwan passed a little too closely.

Safely crossing her feline guard, he gestured to the end of the chaise lounge and asked, “May I?”

Lulu pulled her legs up in silent invitation.

Alwan sat and only then noticed the paper between them on the chair. He picked it up and squinted, the darkness making it hard to read.

Before he had a chance to ascertain what it was, Lulu said, "It's the repair quote."

"Where did you print it?"

"I used the hotel's printing service. I figured it would be easier to read than on my phone. Not that it changes the cost estimate."

Alwan saw what she meant immediately. Though it wasn't anything he couldn't afford, the high four-figure estimate for her repairs garnered a low whistle from him. "That is a hefty sum."

"Apparently, beyond the generator I'll need to buy, there's also an issue with the engine. I was expecting for it to be costly, but it's even worse than I imagined." She laughed bitterly and looked away, back at the realistic flames crackling and snapping in the fireplace.

He knew what was coming, sensed where the conversation was headed, but he needed to hear her say it.

"If…if I agree to your fake engagement, I need you to agree to some stipulations."

Keeping a lid on his joy was challenging, but Alwan schooled his features into neutral as he said, "Anything to make you more comfortable."

"I don't think anything could make me *comfortable* with this," Lulu said dryly.

"And yet still, your comfort matters to me." Because it did.

Despite knowing each other most of their lives, for the first time Alwan felt like he knew her better after learning a bit more about how her divorce had worried her family and eventually led to her solo-traveling in her RV through the Canadian wilderness. Her motor home was clearly important to her in the same way this next step of his career was for him.

For that reason alone, her comfort was now his utmost priority. He would do whatever he could to alleviate any concerns she had before they embarked on this ruse together.

"Shoot. What are your stipulations?"

Lulu took a sip from her mug before she said, "First, to be clear, we can't actually get married. I'm okay with an engagement, but it can't go beyond that."

What she said made perfect sense to him. Alwan didn't actually want to be tied down, and he was betting that after her divorce neither did she. Besides, his parents never specified that he had to be *married*. In this case, a bride-to-be should suffice for all his intents and purposes and satisfy their clause to see him blissfully and—unbeknownst to them—momentarily engaged.

"Deal. There'll be no official papers, and no wedding party as part of our agreement. Is that all?"

"No, we should also have a timeline for when we want to end things. I'm thinking a year. Is that enough time for you to open your practice?"

"A year should be plenty of time, so I'm all right with that."

"Good. Also, when this ends, we let our families down gently together. We'll simply tell them that it just didn't work between us and that we're on the same page with a mutual, amicable breakup."

He cocked his head to the side, studying her for a quiet moment. "Does that part worry you?"

"Doesn't it worry you?" She lifted her brows at him, frowning her incredulity. "I don't want to hurt my family or yours. Even if *we* know this engagement won't be real, it doesn't mean they will. Besides, our parents are friends. This shouldn't cause a rift between them."

"Agreed. Anything else?"

Lulu wrung her hands around her mug, the nervous tell setting off alarms in him, and when she didn't respond immediately his anxiety only shot up higher.

Finally, after a long pause, she said, "Since none of this is real, there shouldn't be any…intimacy." She avoided direct eye contact when she spoke, her shyness more than apparent now.

His relief quickly switched to amusement. Feeling impish suddenly, Alwan teased, "Intimacy?"

"You know what I mean," she said, glancing at him before bowing her head and staring down at her mug as though its contents were fascinating.

"But just so we're clear though, what are we talking is off-limits exactly? Hand-holding, hugging, and kissing—"

"Alwan!"

He held out his hands placatingly and laughed. "All right, I hear you. No PDA of any kind." But not even a few seconds later, he drawled, "So… does that mean no late-night phone calls too?"

Her disapproving glower was swift, and he had to bite the inside of his cheek to keep from laughing.

"Okay, fine. No intimacy, period. Is that it?"

"That's all," she said.

"Good. I have something I'd like to add, then. A final rule we both can probably agree to, but one that still needs to be said, we can't confuse or complicate this with any kind of emotional entanglement."

"You think I'm going to fall in love with you?" Lulu's laughter was loud and unabashed. He should've been offended, but instead, he smiled.

Face glowing from her mirth, she wiped her eyes and laughed again. "Don't worry. That won't be a problem."

He laughed too. "Then we have a deal." Holding up her repair bill, he said, "And as per our agreement, I'll handle this. The only thing left to ask is, when would you like to go ring shopping?"

"Don't worry," Lulu said, looking down at her hand. "I'll have that covered."

Baffled by his disappointment at that news, he tucked aside his strange upset and said, "I guess there are no more roadblocks. We're officially engaged."

"*Fake* engaged."

Alwan simply grinned and said, "Whatever you say, my fake fiancée."

CHAPTER FOUR

LULU HAD ALWAYS known she'd return home to Toronto someday.

She just hadn't ever pictured that when she did, it would be with a fiancé.

Before they'd left Alberta, Alwan had done as he'd promised and paid the deposit on her repair bill for her RV to the mechanic. The remaining cost for the repairs he'd then transferred to her bank account. And with that he'd honored his part of their fake engagement deal.

Now it was her turn to uphold her end of their partnership.

Be his perfect pretend bride-to-be.

On the four-hour flight home, they'd hashed out their approach and gotten their stories straight. They'd decided to tell their families separately, but that had led to three days of nonstop questions, so she was grateful they'd be together with both sets of parents today so that answers could be given and worries soothed.

"Do you love our Luula?" her father asked the

moment Alwan's Maybach pulled away from the curb. He turned in the passenger seat to pin Alwan with a stern look.

Lulu groaned in Somali, "Aabo, please! Stop embarrassing me…"

Her mother swatted her leg and hushed her. "Aamus! Aabahaa dhegayso."

"How can I listen to him when he's being so humiliating, Hooyo?" Lulu complained, crossing her arms and flopping against the back seat only to gasp and jolt upright a second later when her mother gave her a pinch on the thigh. Seeing the warning in her mother's eyes, Lulu rubbed her leg and clamped her lips together.

"We've known you since you were young, son, but still, we have to ask. Don't be offended and please understand that we only want what's best for Lulu."

At a red light, Alwan looked at her father and, in fluent Somali, said, "I understand fully, and I'm not offended at all, adeer." He turned his head forward and his gaze met hers in the rear-view mirror, searing through her. "But your concern is unfounded as I respect and care for your daughter."

She didn't know how long he stared at her, but it was long enough for drivers to begin blaring their horns behind them. If Alwan heard the angry honking, he wasn't doing anything about it.

Finally, just when she thought her lungs would burst from holding her breath, he looked away. Lulu let out a soft, shuddery breath and blinked furiously, her eyes dry from their staring match.

That was the state she was in when they arrived at Alwan's parents' restaurant. Dropping them off first, he peeled off in search of parking in the busy neighborhood. She watched his taillights disappear before turning to find her parents studying her.

"He'll catch up. We should go inside," Lulu announced and, hoping they'd follow, headed briskly for the entrance to the restaurant, a two-story sleek, steel, glass and black marble building. But not soon enough to miss their exchange of silent looks and secretive smiles.

Inside, the restaurant was quiet and warm. Too quiet. Confused, Lulu looked beyond the empty host podium facing the entrance to the open space of empty tables on the first floor. Alwan had said his parents were expecting them, and it was their restaurant, but they weren't anywhere to be seen.

Soft music played on the speakers, so she figured someone had to be in the building, and she soon heard the sound of heels clacking over the colorfully vibrant Moroccan tiles toward them.

A smiling young woman was tying on a half apron as she walked, smoothing her hands over the front of it where the restaurant's name, Al-Nuri, was printed in yellow-gold lettering.

"Ms. Sadiq?" she asked, her cheeks dimpling when Lulu nodded. "You and your parents are expected upstairs. If you'll follow me." Leading them deeper into the restaurant, she directed them into an elevator but didn't follow them in.

Alwan's parents were waiting as soon as the lift doors opened, and the second Lulu stepped out, she found herself wrapped in his mother's perfumed embrace while his father smiled broadly at her.

It was a warmer reception than the one Alwan had gotten from her parents. But her stomach still swooped nervously when Alwan's parents ushered them to a table in the far corner with views of Lake Ontario from the window walls. And once they were all seated, Alwan's mother, Ayaan, and father, Omer, on one end and Lulu tucked between her parents on the U-shaped majlis sofa on the other side, she tensed as all their focus landed on her.

Meeting each of their intent gazes, she smiled weakly, suddenly struck by the realization she was all alone.

So she was on her own when his mother, hand keenly outstretched, asked, "Oh! Is that the engagement ring?"

Embarrassed, Lulu had no choice but to flash

her new accessory to everyone. While they showered her with compliments, she cast a furtive glance at the elevator, her hope flagging when Alwan was still nowhere in sight. She quietly despaired, figuring no one had noticed.

But Ayaan squeezed her hand with a silvery laugh and smile. "Don't worry, Luula. He texted a minute ago that he found a parking spot farther away and that he'd be with us any moment."

Lulu blushed and bowed her head when all the parents laughed then.

And her cheeks still felt hot to the touch when Alwan finally made his reappearance.

Never had Lulu been more relieved to hear the sound of an elevator ding. Her relief was quickly undercut by her annoyance with him for leaving her in the first place. She glared as he strode over in his gleaming Italian leather shoes, his charcoal-gray suit jacket hooked over one of his arms, his hands adjusting his tie before smoothing over the front of his white-and-gray-striped dress shirt. It only irritated her more that he looked so breathtakingly handsome and impeccably put-together.

"Sorry, I'm late," he panted softly when he reached their table, his tawny brown cheeks flushed red.

Hearing his breathlessness sanded off Lulu's frustration with him. It was difficult to hold on to her irritation when she envisioned him running here from wherever he'd parked his car.

Greeting his parents, Alwan gripped his dad on the shoulder and touched his lips to his mother's forehead. "Salaam, Abu. Yumma. I hope I didn't miss anything," he said before squeezing in between his folks and catching Lulu's eyes across the table.

They were now facing each other, and beneath the table she felt the toe of his shoes bump her low, slingback heels. At first she didn't think anything of it, but then he did it again.

Above the table, his lips tilted up in a small smile and he raised an eyebrow at her in silent question.

Touched that he was checking in on her, she smiled back, mollified for the time being.

"You haven't missed anything, Alwan," her mother said and wrapped an arm around Lulu's shoulders. "We have just been wondering how this happened, and since Luula won't tell us, maybe you can. How did you and our Luula fall in love?"

Love? If only they knew...

The only commonality to love that she shared with Alwan was his love for his career and hers for her RV and the solace and peace it had given her during a rough patch in her life. There wouldn't be—*couldn't be*—anything else between them. Not simply because it would ruin their plans, but also because romance and a happy-ever-after were crossed out of her heart and head forever. And even if she was interested, which Lulu most certainly was not, Alwan, with his big ego and fixation on his profession, appeared to be the last person who would have time for a relationship.

Naturally, she had a visceral reaction at the word *love* used in the same sentence with her and Alwan.

Lulu cringed audibly enough for her mom to kiss her teeth.

"What?" her mother asked sharply. "We can't be curious?"

"I know I am!" his mother chimed in with another warm, tinkling laugh.

Their fathers were more silent, but they too nodded in agreement with their wives.

Since the question wasn't posed to her, Lulu sat back and watched Alwan like everyone else. She already knew what he would say, having rehearsed their story enough times over the past few days. All she had to do was nod and smile at the appropriate times, which was an easy enough task.

At least it *was* easy until Alwan said, "I knew Luula had been *wanting* me to propose, so I figured it was time. Why make either of us wait? I didn't want her pining for me anymore..."

Wanting? Pining!

Since *when* did they agree on that narrative?

Shock wearing away quickly, Lulu nudged his foot under the table. Okay, maybe *nudged* wasn't the right verb. More like she stepped on him. Hard. Right on those stupid toes of his in those stupid expensive shoes and watched him jolt in his seat mid-explanation and bite his lip and stifle a pained grunt.

"Alwan, are you all right, habibi?" his mother wondered.

Quietly, he waved off the concern both sets of parents showed.

Serves him right.

But not fully satisfied, and still out for blood, she grabbed the opening to speak her mind. "But that was *after* Alwan cried and told me he couldn't live without me—"

Alwan's hissing intake of air cut her off, but his wide, shocked eyes gave her an unexpected thrill. Childish though it was, and perhaps a little dangerous when he narrowed his eyes at her, Lulu couldn't help goading him with a grin. She held back the urge to stick her tongue out at him. *Two can play at that game.*

"Cried? Really?" his mom repeated softly, touching his arm.

Alwan smiled down at his mother, but his stare bored through Lulu as he gruffly said, "I forgot that part, but if Luula says it happened—"

"It did," she interjected.

"Then I suppose it did," he assented, his eyes unreadable but his mouth lifting with a smile. He could've outed her. But then, she knew, that he'd be outing himself.

After that Alwan answered more faithfully to their practiced script, leaving Lulu with the impression that he'd learned his lesson and wouldn't play with her like that again. Brunch was eventually served, and Alwan's parents helped their staff with the setup, which thankfully pressed Pause on the questioning. Meanwhile Lulu noted her mother and father were chatting more amiably with Alwan. From the look of things, no one suspected they were lying, so she and Alwan were in the clear.

But just when she thought she could let down her guard, a sudden clenching sensation seized her lower belly. It felt like a fist was slowly but firmly squeezing her insides. Lulu tightened her lips on a pained moan and pressed her hands just below her stomach, where the dull ache was centered.

She hoped it was hunger.

Unfortunately, after an hour flew by and most their plates were cleared, Lulu was still quietly suffering, only now the gnawing discomfort dropped lower and seemed more familiar. Not that knowing it was her period made it any better. Her cycles were never regular, so she wasn't surprised that she was caught off guard now.

Her parents were busy chatting with Alwan's mother and father, and Alwan himself was distracted scrolling through his phone. It was the perfect time to excuse herself without an awkward explanation, and having visited his parents' restaurant before, she knew where to find the restroom.

On the way there, and desperate to get her mind off her pain, Lulu admired the African-inspired touches to the restaurant's interior design. Woven shades covered the pendant lights hanging over the gleaming handcrafted wooden tables and chairs, the walls were painted a soft, earthy beige, and colorfully vibrant rugs hung in recessed alcoves. The cultural touches in the decor were as well-thought-out as the flavorful Sudanese and Somali dishes they'd just enjoyed.

It was easy to see that his parents had poured their love into making this restaurant feel like a second home.

Her smile turned into a grimace when another pulsating wave of torment struck.

Hurrying into the washroom, Lulu discovered that she'd forgotten to toss painkillers in her tiny, decorative handheld purse. She set her teeth against the now-nauseating waves of pain and shuffled out into the well-lit hallway. How was it that even walking was hurting her?

God.

She'd barely taken two steps back the way she had come when Alwan's low drawl came from behind her.

"There you are."

Letting out a short squeal, Lulu spun around and gasped, "Alwan!" Irritation surging through her almost immediately, she snapped, "Why do you keep scaring me like that? I'm seriously going to strap a bell to you if you don't stop. Honestly, you're worse than my cat. Even he has the decency to meow and let me know he's there."

He chuckled and slid his hands in his trouser pockets. "Hey, don't blame me if you were too distracted to hear *or* see me. This isn't exactly an ideal hiding spot."

Not ready to admit that she was preoccupied, Lulu settled on quietly glaring at his smiling features. "I'm leaving," she said, but before she could turn away, yet another cresting pain gripped her insides. It was like a white-hot band of agony constricting her middle. And it wouldn't let her go. She hunched over slightly, her arms instinctively wrapping over the front of her. Lulu might've been humiliated that Alwan was still with her, but she was hurting far too much to care.

"Lulu, are you okay?" he asked, his warm, solid presence by her side in a flash.

She shook her head jerkily, focusing on deep breathing through the physical assault on her body.

Hearing Alwan curse under his breath, she closed her eyes and waited for him to panic and rush off to get help from his mother or hers. If he was anything like her ex-husband, Mohamed, that was what he'd have done.

So she was taken aback then when Alwan not only stuck with her but even crouched down low so she could see him.

Once he made eye contact, he asked, "Can you walk?"

Still busy with her belly-breathing exercise, Lulu gave him a curt nod.

The furrows in his brow lessened, his relief sweeping over his handsome face in a bright smile. "All right. That's good news. Though, just so you know, I was fully prepared to carry you if it came down to that."

Lulu snorted. "Duly noted."

Eyes twinkling merrily, Alwan moved toward the end of the hall and stopped when she didn't follow.

"I don't want to go out there yet." She leaned

her head back against the wall, straightening her posture and feeling a reprieve from the shooting pain. Worrying everybody else wouldn't make her feel better. "I just need time. Oh, and ibuprofen."

Alwan looked long and hard at her for a beat before he nodded in understanding. "Then we'll go to the office."

"Why the office?" Lulu asked him.

"If I know my parents, they should have some pain reliever there," Alwan explained, looking back to make sure she was following him.

Leading her down the hall past the restrooms for their guests and beyond the Employees Only sign, Alwan stopped at the door at the end that read Office.

He pulled his keys out of his pocket to unlock the door.

"You carry a key to your parents' office?"

Alwan laughed at the unconcealed suspicion in her tone. "Normally I wouldn't, but my father misplaced his spare once. My parents decided that, given I don't live with them, it was best that I keep the extra key."

"I suppose," she said, rousing another amused chuckle from him.

Inside the small but neatly maintained office, Alwan headed straight for the nondescript desk in the middle and opened its drawers. "The first aid kit should be here somewhere," he mumbled to himself. After opening the first two drawers, he finally struck gold. "Aha. I knew it was here."

Eagerly retrieving the pain reliever from the first aid kit, he raised his head to find Lulu still standing closer to the door. She faced the wall and stared at the few framed photos of his family and his parents' staff members hanging there.

Closing his fist around the bottle in his grasp, Alwan walked over with leaden limbs, keeping his eyes on her. Knowing what the photos already showed, he didn't regard them.

"Luula?"

At the sound of her name, she turned her head to him and noted the bottle in his open palm.

"Let me get you water."

He strode over to the corner of the office where a watercooler was stationed. Filling a small paper cup for her, Alwan walked it back to where she stood. Murmuring her gratitude, her features momentarily twisted into a pained grimace before she opened the bottle, took a pill and washed it down.

"Did you want to sit down?" he asked her when she compressed her lips and squeezed her eyes closed in quiet suffering.

A feeling of helplessness crept over him. He didn't know why he did it, but he flung a glance at the photos on the wall, one in particular sticking out from the collection. Looking away before the darkness clawed into him, Alwan looked back at Lulu and gave her his full attention.

"Actually, I could use fresh air more."

He tossed another quick look at the framed photos. Fresh air sounded good to him right about then too.

Locking up the office, they walked back to where their parents were seated. Before they reached the table, Lulu tapped his arm.

It was a light touch. There and gone. Certainly nothing that should have had him responding instantly by stiffening all over, his body wired tight, his attention at her command.

"Can you not tell them I'm not feeling well?" She looked from their table back to him, rewarding him with a smile when he nodded.

"Where did you two go?" his mother asked him as soon as they were within earshot.

"I was showing Luula around the restaurant, and now we're just going out for some air."

His father pulled his glasses off and furrowed his bushy brows. "It isn't the first time she's been here, Alwan. What were you showing her exactly?"

"Uh, just some family photos in the office."

"Let them go," Lulu's mother, Huda, said kindly. "They're young, in love—"

"And hopefully soon-to-be-wedded," Mahad, Lulu's father, finished with a stern look at Alwan in particular.

Since he wasn't about to argue with her father, Alwan promised, "We'll be right out there on the balcony," and pointed to the long wall of windows letting in a wash of natural light into the restaurant.

With their blessing, Alwan led Lulu away, and folding open the glass doors, he walked her outdoors.

"How are you not dying of embarrassment?" Lulu groaned the instant they were alone.

He grinned and walked with her to the edge of the balcony. "Who says I'm not?"

She appraised him with a sniff. "You look pretty calm to me."

"It's practice," he said, spinning around and leaning against the balcony's guardrail. "When I'm in the courtroom, I have to put on a poker face, even if I know my chances of winning for my client are not in my favor." Alwan nudged his chin toward where their parents were sneaking peeks at them. "It doesn't mean I'm not more than a little worried that they'll try and marry us off sooner."

"Great. Now you're scaring me too," Lulu griped, making him laugh.

Grasping the balcony handrail, she looked

out at the shimmering lake and the Toronto Islands, the chain of well-frequented islands near the city's shores.

"Wow," she uttered quietly.

Having seen it so many times wore off the charm, but he tried to place himself in her shoes and turned back around to cast his gaze over the rippling lake glimmering with the bright white sunlight. The longer he stared the more Alwan began to feel the stirring of a lost appreciation for the cloudless blue sky, the nippy lake-scented breeze brushing his face, and the steady drone of the city he loved all around them.

"I know I've been here before, but I always forget how peaceful it is."

He hummed his agreement, knowing he couldn't add anything since she'd said it so perfectly.

"This is where you and your family took that picture together, isn't it?"

Any serenity Alwan had felt blasted away. Just like that he was back in the office, the photo he'd avoided in there filtering into his mind.

Not now. Not here with her.

He clamped his hands around the railing and, feeling Lulu's eyes on him, forced himself to grit out, "Yeah."

"You all looked so happy. When was it taken?"

Alwan clenched his teeth and a muscle leaped along his jaw.

He knew it wasn't her fault for asking innocent questions. It wasn't like Lulu understood that she was poking at a wound and peeling back a scab that had never fully healed despite years having passed since he'd first gotten the injury. *Since Hashim left.*

Since his big brother walked out of the reputable, private rehabilitation facility their parents had shelled out big money to send him to receive the help he wasn't getting anywhere else. Not the hospitals, self-help groups or the interventions they'd tried staging as a family. Rehab had been their last-ditch effort to drag Hashim out of what they believed was a deep, dark pit of his own making.

What his parents didn't know, what he hadn't told anyone, was that he'd helped Hashim escape. At the time Alwan had thought he had been *saving* his brother, but all he had done was more harm than good.

It secretly made up a big reason why he wanted the fake relationship with Lulu now. Disappointing his parents *again* after everything they'd gone through was all he wanted to avoid.

With great difficulty, he said, "Eighteen summers ago. The day before Hashim left to go to the States for college on a rugby scholarship."

“Right. I almost forgot you had a brother,” Lulu said and looked back out at the lake.

Me too. Alwan squeezed the balcony railing tighter, hating that he had that thought but knowing it was true. Because just as there were moments where all he could think about was where Hashim could be and what his brother could have been possibly up to all this time, there were days that went by where Alwan had gotten caught up in his own life and hadn’t spared one moment for his runaway brother. Guiltily he admitted that he liked the times where he forgot more and more. But it was exhausting thinking of his brother, knowing possibly that Hashim might not ever have spared a thought for him in return.

Of course, it would be easier to forget him if Lulu hadn’t reminded him now.

“I haven’t seen Hashim around in a while,” she observed. “He’s still in Sudan, isn’t he? Has he visited you since then?”

That lie about his brother being with extended family in Sudan was concocted by his parents right after Hashim had disappeared sixteen years ago. Rather than letting everyone know what truly had happened, they’d crafted another narrative. One that they’d kept going for a decade and a half now, but it did the trick and spared them the grief of gossipmongers.

Alwan hadn’t agreed with their decision.

Why should they cover for Hashim all this time when he'd made the unusually cruel choice to abandon them? It wasn't fair that he'd shattered their trust and broken their hearts and left them to pick up the pieces. *Why should we be the ones hurting and hiding how we feel?*

Fueled by that thought, Alwan toyed with the idea of revealing his family's long-guarded secret to Lulu. This way he could finally unburden himself, though only at the cost of betraying his parents.

Is it worth hurting Abu and Yumma?

Picturing their heartbreak when they learned he divulged the truth cooled his blood. And, in the end, he decided to keep quiet…as always.

"He hasn't visited, and I don't really know what he's been doing. He actually hasn't spoken to any of us in a while. We had a falling-out… of sorts."

Alwan waited for Lulu to ask more questions, or at the very least offer her condolences.

She surprised him when instead she said, "Well, at least you don't have to worry about lying to him."

He blinked his confusion.

"It wasn't hard to lie to my parents," she explained, "but when I told Ladna and Liban, I could almost sense them feel that I was lying my face off."

Hearing that about her sister and brother pulled a small smile from him.

"Why do I get the feeling you're jealous that I'm not speaking with my brother?"

She shrugged. "I'm probably a terrible person, but yes. I kinda am."

Shaking his head, Alwan let out a soft laugh. *Unbelievable.* He didn't know what shocked him more: that Lulu had made light of what he had told her, or that he was struck by the oddest urge to pull her in and hug her for it. Because the darkness that always seemed to crowd in with thoughts of his brother scuttled back at the first sound of his laughter.

Because of her.

Again, he fought the instinct to embrace her, the immense relief and gratitude he felt lodging in his throat. But he couldn't say more without risking her finding out the truth about Hashim, so he looked away and hooked his arms over the guardrail beside her.

"It goes without saying that I hope you and your brother work it out."

Her kind words made it that much more of a challenge to bite his tongue. Needing them to move past this, he hoarsely thanked her and said, "Don't be too jealous of me. I had my own problems lying to Malek."

"I thought you said your cousin knew about

you going to Alberta. That he helped cover for you with your parents."

"He did," Alwan said, his elbow brushing her hand on the railing as he leaned in closer to her and whispered the rest, in case their parents were eavesdropping. "I just don't want him knowing any of this is fake. Malek and I, we're close. Because of that, like your brother and sister, it was hard getting him to even believe in all of this."

"It's hard, isn't it? Lying to them," Lulu said with a fluttery, tired-sounding sigh.

"It is, but it's best that we keep this between us. Remember, this is how we get what we want. Your RV. My business."

She frowned but nodded, now anxiously twisting the ring on her left finger.

"Speaking of keeping things between us, is that the engagement ring I'm supposed to have given you?"

Lulu stopped fidgeting immediately and, covering a hand over the ring, looked down, mumbling, "Maybe."

"May I?" He held out his hand.

"Are you going to break one of our conditions already? No unnecessary physical contact, remember?"

Alwan felt his lips kick up, amusement coursing warmly through him. "That won't be a problem if you allow me." And then because he sensed she'd approve, he added, "Please."

That appeared to do the trick because Lulu slowly, cautiously placed her hand in his upturned palm. Though she held her fingers still in his grasp, her nervousness was apparent. She had her glossy bottom lip tucked between her teeth and her head turned to the side, though Alwan didn't miss her peeks every now and again when she thought he wasn't looking.

Curling his fingers gently around her hand, he lifted her ring up closer to the light, the sun glinting off the larger cubic zirconia in the center of a circle of similar but far smaller stones. Not that he was a jeweler, but as pretty as the silver band was around her finger, Alwan knew he could've given her something far less…simple. *Cheap.*

A ring that better matched her beauty.

With Lulu looking away, he found a rare opportunity to study her and he didn't squander it, drinking her in shamelessly.

She'd dressed up for the meeting between their parents. Her shoulder-length dark hair drawn up into a tidy bun with two thick tendrils coiling down from her temples, her makeup only enhancing her glowing, warm reddish-brown skin. The long-sleeved black jumpsuit she wore was as sparkly as her gold chandelier earrings, and gone were her hiking boots, replaced by a pair of kitten heels that weren't as dainty as their suede appearance belied. His poor toes could attest to it.

She looked different, but not in the way that made her unrecognizable. Still enticingly pretty to him no matter how she appeared or what she wore.

And the ring was her choice, so he'd respect it.

She must have felt his stare because Lulu turned her head back to him and asked, "Do you not like it?"

"Would you change it if I said so?"

Without missing a beat, she breathed, "No."

"Then," he rasped, "it's perfect."

Just like this arrangement could be for them, so long as Alwan kept his emotions in check and Lulu did the same.

CHAPTER FIVE

ALWAN WAS BEGINNING to believe that the reason he wasn't already married was because he'd suspected just how exhausting wedding planning could be. And even though he wasn't really getting married, that fact didn't exempt him from the tortuous activity of venue searching with his parents and Lulu's.

It had all started when the subject of not finding a suitable venue in time came up in conversation.

What if all the good places are booked up? his mother had said.

We should help them look, Lulu's mother had then suggested.

To keep up appearances, he and Lulu had no choice but to agree and be hauled along for the search.

The only upside was that he had her to commiserate with.

And from the amount of times Lulu flung him comical looks that said she'd rather be anywhere else as they strolled the newly blooming garden grounds of the famed, historic Casa Loma, Alwan safely guessed that she wasn't happy either.

Unlike him though, she was faking her good mood far easier than he ever could.

"I thought the library and conservatory were beautiful, but this pavilion is lovely," she gushed at one point when her parents and his looked to them for their opinions. Despite the grand Gothic Revival castle being the third venue that they'd visited already that day alone, and all by noon, Lulu smiled brilliantly and said all the right things to please his parents and her mother and father.

With her doing all the heavy lifting, all he had to do was trail closely by her side and nod and beam on cue.

When the tour finally, joyfully, came to an end, the venue staff member showing them around guided them to the pavilion's exit. Their parents followed, chattering excitedly, and as Alwan began to stalk after them, already dreading the next venue they likely planned to drag him and Lulu to, he noticed that his bride-to-be wasn't by his side any longer.

Looking back, he didn't have to search far for her.

Bathed in the sunlight pouring in from the pavilion's glass roof, Lulu stood still and stared up transfixed at the mansion's towering turret and stony exterior.

"Luula, everyone's left," he said, walking up to her.

She blinked over at him as though she'd lost track of time.

But that wasn't what robbed him of his breath temporarily. With the light outdoors brightening her brown eyes, he saw clear as the sunny day outside a longing in her gaze that went beyond the power of any words in any language on this planet. So palpable was that yearning, it eked a shiver out of him before a strange pining to give her what she quietly desired squeezed his chest.

"You like this place." He knew he didn't have to say it, but she confirmed it when she looked back up at the castle.

"It's stunning, how could I not?"

Alwan surveyed the impressive pavilion, seeing exactly why she was taken with the naturally lit space with its touches of indoor greenery, all glass walls and roof, charcoal-stained cedar flooring and sparkling crystal chandeliers hanging from the metal rafters. Still, it wasn't anything he hadn't seen before. Though he couldn't recall specifics from having attended countless work-related gatherings, Alwan swore he'd dined in a similar pavilion. *Maybe even this very one*, he mused. Not to mention he had lost track of the times his parents had dragged him to one of their boring business networking soirees, from silent dinner auctions to ballroom charity galas, and all hosted in elegant venues just like this one.

Of course *now* in hindsight he wished he'd hobnobbed more with Toronto's upper-crust, networked on his own without his parents' intervention, and spared both him and Lulu this marriage charade. Still, as hard as it was for him to smile and lie while looking his family and hers in the eye, Alwan could only imagine what it was like for her.

All of this had to be reminding her of her divorce.

And that knowledge made him feel like a heel. *She's getting something out of this deal too.* But even though she'd benefited by taking his money, it didn't make him feel any better.

Rather than pretend like he was thinking about anything else, he asked, "Is this the kind of venue you had for your first marriage?"

She gave a light snort. "Hardly. Our budget was modest, so the event space was smaller. Weren't you there? I certainly recall seeing your parents—they gave generously to my wedding money box."

"No, sorry, I missed out. And yeah, that sounds like them." He said the last part with a proud smile. The one trait he'd always admired was how readily his mother and father swooped to the aid of others, whether it was for extended family or a stranger they had met only once, they were openhanded to a fault. But that was where the power of their compassion ended because even with their millions, his parents couldn't prevent Hashim from running away and leaving them—

Leaving me *behind.*

But this wasn't about his brother, and training his sights back on Lulu, he smiled to mask the darker path his thoughts had taken.

"Were you happy with your wedding? I know little girls dream of their big day, so the expectation had to be set high."

"Oh, and little boys don't?" she taunted with a quick smile.

He grinned and shrugged. "Hey, blame society's gender stereotyping. But if you're asking me specifically, no, I never really dreamed about getting married."

"Not even a little bit?"

"Not in the least. Always seemed like a lot of pressure, and after today, I know my gut instinct's proven. Weddings are a lot of work and certainly not for the faint of heart." And that was saying plenty given he'd sat through his rigorous bar exam and the grueling hours of studying and prep work required for it. Still, he would rather do that all over again than plan a wedding anytime soon. Lucky for him, all of this with Lulu was make-believe.

Alwan didn't know what he'd do if it were actually real.

If we were really getting married.

Staring down at her lovely side profile, he blinked out of his momentary stupor when Lulu suddenly strolled away from him, through the open doors of the pavilion and into the estate gardens.

"Where are you going?" he called after her before hurrying to catch up.

"For a walk," she replied, her strides slow and carefree as she walked the cobbled path from the pavilion onto the green, well-kept lawn. Drawing her wavy dark hair from her face, she looked back over her shoulder at him and asked, "Are you coming?" Even though she extended the invitation, he had the feeling that either way Lulu seemed determined to take a stroll with or without him.

Glancing around, Alwan followed.

As soon as he fell into step with her, she said, "One thing I've discovered is that a happy wedding doesn't guarantee a happy marriage. Sometimes a fairy tale is just meant for a storybook."

"Was it that bad? Your divorce?" Normally he wouldn't have dared to be so nosy, but there was something about the way she looked just then—sad yet resigned to the fate of her previous relationship—that hooked its claws into him. But considering it wasn't any of his business, Alwan was prepared for her to ignore him, possibly even snap his head off.

Instead of doing either of those things, she bowed her head. "It was…tough. I think it ending was the best for both of us, but obviously most people marry thinking it'll be for a lifetime. At least that's the hope, and we trust it, but sometimes that trust is misplaced."

"That's why I haven't married yet," he said.

Alwan swallowed when her eyes locked onto his. This wasn't where he envisioned their once-harmless conversation heading, but after witnessing her unexpected vulnerability, it not only seemed fair to reciprocate—it felt oddly *right* to do.

"I find it hard to trust others easily, and before you ask, it isn't because a woman tore my heart out and ripped it to shreds. I've been this way for as long as I can remember." He could've left it there. Possibly *should* have, but under Lulu's watchful gaze, the urge to tell her more pressed in on him, squeezed in from all sides until he burst.

"I told you about how my brother cut communication off with my parents and me. What

I didn't tell you is that his silence has made it harder for me to trust others and I resent him for it," he said, speaking so fast, his tongue tripped over some of the words. Breathing deeply, he tried and failed to ease the anxiety tightening his muscles and adrenaline priming him to flee.

Rather than running though, Alwan glanced away from Lulu to the fountain they were standing beside and waited for the regret to slam into him.

For his brain to scream that he'd made a big mistake, and then push him to retract everything he'd just said. *Lie to her. Tell her that none of what I said is true. That I'm not as pathetic as I just made myself out to be.*

"Alwan?" Lulu called to him, her voice rising above his nagging thoughts.

He forced himself to turn his head back to her. And what he expected he didn't see. The pity that he'd been so sure would be present wasn't there. She had nothing but a smile for him, small but full of compassion and sympathy.

"Trust isn't an easy thing to hold, and it's even harder to give away," she said softly, soothing his soul in a way she'd never know…not unless he told her, and he'd said enough today.

Curiously, the weight in his chest he'd grown accustomed to for so long had shifted. *Shrunk*, he realized in shock.

He was lighter. Not entirely freed of the burden tied to the memories of his brother, but no longer shackled all over either. He had Lulu to thank for it.

The irony that he'd *trusted* her with his feelings wasn't lost on him.

Alwan had always thought Lulu was the best option for a fake fiancée for the sole reason that she'd never get swept up in their lies and fall in love with him. But now he was wondering if there was more to his selecting her…

Don't go there.

None of this was real, and pretending otherwise would only end in the kind of trouble and grief he was trying to avoid all along by choosing Lulu.

Needing more of a reminder, he gazed up at the gushing waters of the fountain and said, "I'm doing this because I don't want to hurt my parents too. Everything I'm doing is just to make all of us happy. I don't want them to worry about me…"

"But they *will* be worried, even if we do our best to reassure them that neither of us holds hurt feelings and the decision to end things was mutual. It's just what parents do," she said quietly.

Steel shooting through his jaw, Alwan lowered his head and leveled his eyes on her. "That may be true, but hopefully by that point I should have a successful legal practice. Then I'll tell them the truth, that I have no interest in marriage. At least that way their disappointment might be mitigated."

"Why do I get the feeling that you've thought all of this out from the beginning, even before you considered coming to me with your plan," she observed and raised her brows expectantly.

He flashed her a smile. "Perhaps I did." Before he could say more, his phone buzzed in his pocket. Excusing himself, he regarded the incoming notification and smiled wider, the news in his inbox timely.

"You look pleased," she said, walking away from the fountain to a bench nearby, the blossoming cherry tree beside it offering shady shelter from the midday early May sun. Brushing the pale pink petals off the bench, she sat down and smoothed her hands over her sleeveless white blouse and down the front of her long, belted, denim skirt.

Taking the seat beside her, Alwan said, "Definitely pleased. I'm officially a free agent as of this very moment. Which means that nothing's holding me back from moving forward with my business plans." Quitting his job had been the last obstacle over the past couple weeks since he and Lulu had returned to Toronto, and now that he'd cleared his exit interview with HR, he could put all his drive and passion into opening the doors on his own practice.

Just another thing he owed to Lulu. If she hadn't agreed to this fake engagement, he'd never have considered quitting so soon and so confidently.

And he was beyond appreciative.

Maybe that explained what he was feeling now. Because the longer he stared at her, the more a new kind of heat trickled through his bloodstream. He was already leaning in when he stopped himself forcibly, fastening his fingers around the seat of the bench and using it to ground him, his mind reeling from the powerful, mind-numbing instinct to *kiss* her.

He didn't even want to think about what would've happened had he not gotten control of himself at the last moment.

Mistake narrowly averted, and feeling Lulu's curious eyes on him, Alwan cleared his throat and pasted on a confident smile. He needed to remember that this was temporary. All of it, but most especially his confusing attraction to her. And what better way to remind himself then by diving headlong into the very reason he sought her out.

"Now that my schedule is freer, how would you like to help me find an office for my new business?"

* * *

Lulu was tired and annoyed of being carted all over Toronto to different buildings and venues for a wedding that wouldn't ever be happening. But she wasn't upset at all when Alwan had asked for her assistance in scouting an office for his business venture, even though their search entailed much the same thing.

She supposed the difference was that his goal to establish a business was real.

Our engagement isn't.

It was why she reasoned it was in her best interest to help him. The sooner he set up his practice, the quicker they could end their relationship ruse and move on. Closing this weird, wild ride of a chapter of her life was her sole motivation—

Or that was what Lulu had tried to convince herself all of this was really.

If she was being honest though, deep down she'd just wanted to help Alwan. His professionalism was admirable. His passion for his career inspiring. The fact he had left a prestigious law firm and what was likely a fat paycheck spoke to her on a level most people might not have understood and certainly couldn't appreciate. That *she* might not have gotten until she'd completely flipped her own life a year ago.

He was taking a big risk. The kind that could hurt him…and not just his pocketbook.

Despite their past, and the annoyance that she'd been roped into his engagement scheme, Lulu wasn't heartless enough to let him flounder on his own. By lending a hand, helping out even in this small way, she could be evening out his odds in his business crashing and burning before it even took flight.

Don't lie. You liked him asking for your help.

Lulu quietly admitted that there was that too. Given their not-so-friendly history and past childhood rivalry, she wouldn't have ever imagined that Alwan would value her opinion let alone request it for something that he'd made clear was important to him.

She was still surprised and touched that he had three days and a dozen properties later.

"Now, I know I said this about *all* the other places we've looked at, but I promise this is the one!" the real estate agent announced cheerfully as he walked them down the short hall to the latest space that he was showing them.

"Let's hope it is," Alwan whispered to her, his fatigue unmistakable.

She couldn't blame him. They'd been run off their feet pretend-wedding-planning ever since they'd arrived back to the city together. And if that wasn't enough, Lulu had returned to her job as a staffing consultant at her old recruitment agency. It was her first time working since her yearlong personal leave.

Alwan, on the other hand, had picked up work as a volunteer lawyer for a local youth-serving nonprofit associated with their community masjid. He'd had plenty on his plate, and the fact that he was also generously donating his time, knowledge and skills not only impressed her—it *left* an impression on her. The kind that had her wanting to step up and help him scratch finding an office off his to-do list.

"Isn't it something?" the agent asked, all smiles, before launching into his pitch for the space.

As the agent pointed out key selling points, Lulu admired the large windows and glass partitions on all the three smaller offices, which allowed an uninterrupted flood of natural light into the space. The sunlight was bright on the plain white walls and light gray vinyl flooring, the ceilings high and with exposed ductwork that gave it an industrial feel. The top-notch air-conditioning allayed the heat from the sun's bright rays.

If it had been her choice she would've signed the lease on the space right then and there.

Turning his head this way and that, Alwan surveyed the office space slowly, methodically.

Until he finally looked back at her with an unreadable expression and then over at the agent.

"Do you mind giving us a moment to speak?"

Once the agent's shiny leather loafers clacked to the exit and the door closed behind him, Alwan asked her, "Well, what's your honest opinion?"

"I could ask you the same question," she said. "It's not like what *I* think is the deciding factor."

He frowned, looking adorably perplexed. "But it is. That's why I wanted your help."

He stared at her with large, dark eyes, and she was struck by how lost and overwhelmed he appeared.

Sympathy moved her into gently saying, "Alwan, I can't make the decision for you. It…it wouldn't be right. Trust me, you want to be the one choosing where you'll be working from to get your clients the justice they're seeking. Not anybody else. *You.*"

"It sounds like you're talking from experience." He crossed his arms, his eyes piercing through the normal shields she held up to the world.

Lulu pulled in a slow breath, anxiety clanging loudly in her head as the conversation turned back on her. Her initial thought was to shut it down and move them back onto the subject of Alwan making his own decisions. But instead of doing that, she said, "When I first considered traveling, it was more of a fantasy I'd play in my head every now and again. A fun daydream to get me through the day.

"After my divorce, the fantasy played nonstop on loop, and that was when I finally decided I'd have to do something about it."

"You bought the motor home," he said with an understanding nod.

"I'd taken half my savings out to do it, then used the rest to budget my expenses on the road."

Lulu swallowed dryly, recalling that nerve-racking moment of her life when she'd put not only money on the line, but all of her hope. It had been one of her toughest choices to leave her work, her friends and family, and everything else she knew and loved in Toronto in the rear-view mirror. And she'd had good cause to be concerned because it hadn't been easy being a traveler. There were skills, like doing light maintenance work on her RV, that she had to learn on the go. Terrifying moments like being caught in a powerful storm current in the wilderness that had her questioning her sanity in choosing that path. And then there was the doubt… That small but loud part of her that wondered whether the RV and road-tripping wasn't all just an excuse for her to run away from her real-world problems.

Problems like her failed marriage…

And any chance of starting my own family.

Lulu hugged her arms around her middle, her heart as heavy as the thoughts packed in her head. She shook most of them away when Alwan spoke up, pretended like her mind hadn't been steeped in dark sorrow for a minute there.

"It must have lived up to the fantasy though, otherwise you wouldn't have been gone for a year, and you wouldn't be thinking of going back. You *are* still going back?"

Funny. Now that he asked, she wasn't so sure about her plans moving forward when her motor home was repaired. And considering she'd only signed up to this engagement charade of his to secure the money for repairs, it made that revelation all the more ground-shaking.

But reminding herself that they weren't standing around there for her, Lulu forced a smile and nodded, hoping that was enough since she didn't think she could lie to his face right then.

"So, the moral is I should trust my gut and go with the choice that's best for me at this moment?"

"Pretty much," she said with feigned cheer.

Lowering his arms from where they were crossed over his chest, Alwan blew a loud breath, his frustration turning down his mouth and etching frown lines over his brow. Swiping his face with both his palms, he groaned, "I wish it made this easier." He heaved another long sigh. "I guess the only way over is straight through. I'm just worried about…" He trailed off, turning his head to the windows and the flood of sunlight streaming into the office space. Stroking at his short beard thoughtfully now, he continued, his voice lower, hoarser, "To be honest, I sometimes wonder if I might not have made a mistake. What if nothing comes from any of this, quitting my job, striking it out on my own…even this ruse with you."

Lulu's breath hitched when he looked back at her.

"What if it amounts to absolutely nothing? What then? Not only will I have let myself down, I'll have disappointed my family, and… and wasted your time with this partnership."

"I can't make you feel better about anything else, but I *can* say that not once have I considered our arrangement a 'waste of my time.'"

He raised his brows and his smile made a re-appearance. "You're not just saying that to make me feel better?"

"When have I *ever* gone out of my way to make you feel better?"

"Good point," he laughed, the gusty, unfettered sound of it filling the whole room and fizzing through her. Unable to fight it any longer, Lulu joined in his laughter until his phone interrupted them.

"It's my mom," Alwan said with a small frown. "She and my dad are usually busy with the restaurant this time of day. I hope nothing's wrong."

"The only way you'll find out is by answering," Lulu encouraged.

With a short nod, he did just that. "Salaam, Yumma."

The conversation was short, and mostly in Arabic, but Lulu sensed a friction from the one side she could hear. It only grew more pronounced by the end of the conversation when Alwan grunted, "Yeah, okay. Salaams to you and Abu both. Yes, I'll tell her you said hello."

"What happened?" she blurted, too intrigued to even pretend like she wasn't invested in whatever had transpired between Alwan and his mother.

"Nothing good," he muttered.

Lulu's chest squeezed, her curiosity morphing into apprehension.

"First off, my mom says 'hi,'" Alwan informed her, sighing sharply. "And the reason she called was because tomorrow she'd like us to visit a venue that a friend of hers owns and rents out for events. Apparently, this friend of hers has had a date suddenly open up and is desperate to fill it."

"What's so bad about that?"

"That date that's opened up? It's just about four months from now, on Labour Day."

"Oh, I see." That explained why he'd gotten so worked up about it.

"Don't worry," Alwan assured her. "I already told her we won't do it."

"Why not?"

Eyes widening and his brows snapping up, Alwan said, "Because four months isn't anywhere near the one-year timeline we agreed on to do *this*." He pointed to the cheap but pretty ring on her finger, prompting her to toy with it.

"I know that, and I get at the time that it seemed like a year was what we needed, but do we feel that way now?"

It wasn't like there were very many obstacles in their path. He had quit his job, and they had spent the last few days searching the city high and low for a suitable workspace for him to run his business from. At this rate, it wouldn't be long before he opened the doors on his practice. And by that point, their fake relationship would've come to a natural end. So if that end happened earlier than planned, wouldn't that be even better?

Only Alwan didn't look like he was happy at all.

His scowl darkened his brooding features, his voice a rumble like warning thunder when he said, "It's too soon."

"Four months is quick, yes," she conceded,

hastening to add, "*but* hear me out, what if you had your practice ready to go by then?" When she saw his brows knit together, she was hopeful he was considering it.

That hope died when Alwan suddenly sealed the distance between them in a few short strides. Evidently, he had something else on his mind now.

With no time to back away, she stood her ground and peered up at him, his sun-bright brown eyes drowning her in their beauty. Every part of her attuned to his larger-than-life presence, only made more prominent now that he'd gotten up close and personal with her. There wasn't a part of Lulu that Alwan didn't affect. His musky, spicy cologne poured into her lungs and his body heat had her wondering where the AC that had been working just fine up until that point had gone.

She stood motionless when Alwan raised his hand and held it hovering by her cheek, the question in his narrowed eyes clear.

She shouldn't even be thinking it.

Should definitely be walking—no, *running* away from the electrified chemistry sparking between them. A chemistry that absolutely shouldn't exist, and shouldn't be wreaking havoc on her senses and driving out all sensibility from her brain.

We can't.

We really, really *shouldn't.*

But she was, swaying into him, following her instincts completely just like she had when she'd impulsively purchased her RV and then again when she had agreed to Alwan's proposal to be fake lovers. This didn't have to be any different…

Not when all the things in her life that had been carefully thought-out decisions—her marriage and dream to have children—had never panned out the way she had hoped.

If she'd learned anything from her reckless choices, it was that they had worked best for her and ultimately given her the most joy in her life.

And why should it be different with Alwan?

So, without a thought or care for anything but wanting to feel him, Lulu leaned into his big palm and closed her eyes, her face as warm as his hand. And when a sigh fluttered from her lips, she opened her eyes and found him staring at her with heated approval, his thumb caressing her cheek, his smile slow and seductive.

"We're breaking our no-touching rule again, but it feels good, doesn't it?"

She rolled her eyes and mumbled, "Don't ruin it," smiling when Alwan's throaty chuckle set her pulse racing.

"Fine. Let's move up the timeline." He stroked

her cheek gently. "But only on the condition that you'll keep helping me."

"All right," she said, eyes closed again, experiencing his soft caresses more viscerally that way, as if his touch was everywhere at once. Lulu could've snuggled her cheek into his hand forever.

Unfortunately, she only had another few minutes before the door to the room clicked open and familiar-sounding clacking shoes came down the short hall. By the time the agent was in view, the only evidence that anything had happened between them was Alwan's toothy grin and her sudden fascination with her shoes.

None the wiser, the agent launched into trying to close them on the property. "The final decision is yours, of course, but I strongly advise that you might not find a better price or a better office—"

"You're right," Alwan cut in, looking toward Lulu and flashing her another sultry smile. "I'll take it."

CHAPTER SIX

AS DISPLEASED AS Alwan was about his parents pushing for the wedding date to be moved up, he was far unhappier that he had to yet again endure a venue tour.

Going to one more of these will kill me, he thought, not certain if he was being serious or not.

But with the way his feet ached in his new slip-on leather loafers, and the summerlike temperature baked him in his lightweight polo shirt, pale blue blazer and tan-colored chinos, Alwan had to assume he might not have been exaggerating completely. Especially when the unseasonably hot wind picked up and it started lightly raining.

The threat of a storm was all the more reason for him to end the tour of the multi-acreage country estate as soon as he was able.

"We'll take it," he announced to Hawa, their tour guide and the owner's twentysomething daughter from what he'd gathered at the beginning of the little excursion.

Recovering from her shock quickly, she smiled brightly and looked between him and Lulu. "Wonderful! If you're decided on a Labour Day wedding, then I'll just have you follow me to the back where we'll fill out some paperwork and accept your deposit."

As Hawa forged ahead, likely moving fast so as they didn't change their minds, Alwan heeded Lulu's pointedly judgy stare.

"What? I didn't see a point of wasting any of our time. It's not like we're actually getting married."

She sucked her teeth. "That's my whole point. We're not getting married, so you could've waited for the tour to end. Now it looks suspicious that you agreed to a venue that neither of us have seen fully. Let's just hope your mother's friend doesn't suspect anything." Then lowering her voice, she grumbled, "I already feel bad about booking a venue for a wedding that won't ever happen."

Alwan smiled sheepishly, though the damage was already done. Hawa ushered them into her office and handed them a couple different forms to read through and fill out together to secure their reception at the venue. Lulu took charge of that, but her irritation with him was palpable.

After the paperwork was done, all that was left was for Alwan to pay the deposit.

Once the payment went through, Hawa beamed

and bounced up out of her chair, telling them that her mother would love to congratulate them personally and that she'd fetch her.

"I can see why she's so happy, that deposit had a lot more zeroes than I expected it to. I'll pay you back half of it," Lulu said when they were alone.

He shook his head immediately. "No, you won't. It's the least I can do for rushing through the tour…and I'm not above using the money as a bribe to get you not to be upset with me anymore. So, did it work?"

Alwan only relaxed when Lulu gave him one of her patented eye rolls and finally smiled, her rosy brown cheeks lifting with the gesture, her deep berry purple lip stain popping up against her white teeth and complimenting the warm undertone of her gleaming skin. She'd dressed in a dark tan tunic and trendy mom jeans, the choice of loose-fitting clothing doing little to hide her naturally curvy figure from his suddenly hungry gaze. He raked his eyes over her from her plain white tennis shoes to the top of her curly ponytail, realizing that standing side by side, it almost looked as if they'd purposefully matched outfits…

…like a real couple might have done.

A week ago, that thought might have freaked him out. Now Alwan simply let it sit and marinate in his mind quietly. Before he could make heads or tails of how he felt, Hawa returned with her mother.

"Mr. Eltahir, Ms. Sadiq," she said, "this is my mother, Gisma."

Stylishly dressed in a colorful thobe complete with a matching scarf, and speaking a torrent of arabiyyah with a sprinkling of English here and there, the older Sudani woman embraced them both and every so often would pinch their cheeks affectionately with her henna-tipped fingers.

And that wasn't even the most embarrassing part. He was glad Lulu only understood a handful of Arabic words. It spared him some humiliation.

Smiling and nodding his way through the conversation, he breathed a sigh of relief when Hawa intervened by reminding her mother they had other appointments.

Outside, the weather had taken a turn for the worse, the rain now pouring. Since Alwan had parked his car a little farther down the long drive, Gisma and Hawa offered to fetch umbrellas and wouldn't take a refusal of their hospitality.

Alone once more, Lulu rubbed the cheek Gisma had squeezed and asked, "What were they saying? You looked like you wanted the ground to swallow you whole."

He tipped his head at her amusedly. "Are you sure you want to know?"

"Would I have asked if I didn't?"

"Okay, just don't say I didn't warn you," he cautioned before translating, his face heating up as he did. "Gisma was offering us a blessing, wishing us many grandchildren—'enough to fill a whole house,' specifically." Alwan laughed nervously and avoided looking at Lulu directly as he spoke. Though when she remained silent, he glanced over at her and swore ice pooled into his veins despite the oppressive humidity in the air.

Standing still, Lulu gazed through him, her eyes on him but he could tell she wasn't seeing him. She probably wasn't even *with* him mentally.

"Lulu, what's wrong?" he called, raising his voice to be heard over the rain pounding the pavement.

When she didn't respond, Alwan waved his hand before her face.

She blinked, visibly startling, but the glassiness to her stare was, thankfully, gone.

"Hey, are you okay?"

She didn't answer, just gazed ahead at the long driveway with that distant look in her eyes and bit her lip. Just as he noticed her chin trembling, Lulu started forward, stepping out from under the cover of the porch and striding into the heavy rainfall.

"Lulu!"

He pursued, the whole world fading away as he locked his sights on her fleeing form.

Nothing else mattered to him right then.

Nothing but her.

His heart pounding, Alwan saw Lulu heading for his car and he unlocked the doors so neither of them had to be caught out in the rain for any longer than they'd already been. Not that it mattered. They were both soaking. And normally he'd have cared about what that would mean for his car's premium leather seats, but right then what concerned him more was what happened to have made Lulu take off the way she'd just had.

Was it something I said?

Knowing that he wouldn't get the answer any other way, Alwan shifted in his seat to look at her fully. He was stung when Lulu quickly turned her head away and looked out through her window, her arms folded over her chest, her body language closed off.

Fine, he thought petulantly, *if she wants to be like that...*

With a hardened jaw, he asked, "Why'd you run, Luula?" When she didn't respond, he curled his hands into fists atop his thighs and forced himself to breathe until he was calmer. Whatever was going on with her wouldn't be helped by his anger. Especially not if he wanted to get her to relax and trust him enough to open up.

And though Alwan didn't understand why, he wanted her trust.

He could *feel* her emotional pain. Recognized it in the way her shoulders hunched and she banded her arms tighter around herself.

He had a flash of a similar scenario, only instead of Lulu seated beside him, it was Hashim.

Rankled by the comparison, Alwan shook that memory out of his head as fast as it resurfaced and before it played fully.

"I can't help you if you don't tell me what's wrong," he softly reasoned with her.

Lulu turned her head slowly back to him.

After staring at him for a while, she murmured, "If you want to help me, then drive. Please."

Shoulders sagging from the letdown, he clenched his teeth and forced an exhale out through his nose. But he did as she asked, started the engine, set the wipers on high and drove away from the picturesque country estate.

Driving through the storm required all his concentration, which, lucky for Lulu, meant that he was too preoccupied keeping them safely on the freeway to grill her on her odd behavior. Though Alwan planned to as soon as he was able. Until then, all he could do was eagerly anticipate that moment as they sat in silence through the first half of the two-hour drive back to Toronto.

When the rain finally did let up, the sun even

breaking through the gray clouds, Alwan flung her a quick look and broached the subject again.

"I want to know what happened." No asking this time. No more pleading with her. He deserved an answer, even a vague one. Anything to plug up his worry for her and keep it from spilling out and causing him trouble. Again, he had a flash of his brother's face. Wringing his hands over the smooth leather of the steering wheel, he kept his eyes forward and waited for her to speak.

And waited.

It was only when Alwan had finally accepted that she might not respond, that Lulu whispered, "I'm sorry."

He snapped his head to her, brows raised and voice gruff with confusion. "For?"

"It's not…*easy* for me."

He pressed his lips tightly together and forced himself to simply listen. He sensed Lulu had more to say.

Sure enough, she sighed a soft, shaky note and, for a brief moment, their eyes collided.

"I had a miscarriage— *Alwan!*"

Lulu shrieked his name and pointed ahead to the car that had seemingly come from nowhere and merged in front of him. Arm flinging out to protect her, Alwan braked in time, bringing them to a screeching halt. There was a blaring of horns directly behind him, but no terrifying sound of metal crunching against metal.

Collision evaded, he whipped his head back to her and looked to where she was holding on to the arm he'd used to shield her.

Lulu stared back with wide, petrified eyes.

"You're not hurt?" he asked, feeling her hands squeeze his forearm and breathing in relief when she shook her head slowly. But the solace of knowing she was safe didn't last long.

How could he feel any comfort once he quickly remembered why he'd nearly rear-ended another vehicle?

Learning of her miscarriage had been such a shock that Alwan had taken his eyes off the road and almost sent them both to the hospital.

Though now it made sense. Why she'd run after he'd told her what Gisma had said about them having kids. Even though they both knew this relationship was a mere transactional exchange between them, it didn't mean that being reminded of children when she'd gone through such a loss wouldn't hurt.

"Lulu… I…" He didn't know what to say to her.

Didn't have the first clue as to whether his condolence was even acceptable at this point, or whether his sympathy would only cause more harm than good.

Throat clogged with emotion, Alwan clenched his jaw to hold back his useless words and just stared back at her, frozen with his helplessness.

"I don't want to talk about it, please. I just… I wanted you to know." She lowered her hands from his arm and looked out the window.

Registering the cacophony of car horns behind him, Alwan stiffly turned his head back to the road and got the car moving again, figuring that it was the only way he could be of use to her right then.

Even if he wished that weren't the case.

Between planning a wedding and trying to get his business plans on track, Alwan should've had more than plenty on his plate.

He certainly shouldn't have been obsessing over Lulu like it was his full-time job. What she did outside their fake engagement pact wasn't any of his business, and he was wholly aware of that before she'd agreed to their deal.

Besides, she didn't seem to care what he was doing. Alwan hadn't seen her since he'd dropped her off at her home after their visit to the country estate venue.

That had been three days ago.

He tried reaching out to her on several occasions, but outside a succinct text or two, Lulu had made it clear that she'd wanted her personal space. And Alwan didn't mind giving it to her, but he wondered if she had needed the break from *him* specifically.

After all, she'd trusted him enough to tell him about her miscarriage. And though Lulu had said nothing more, Alwan was honored that she had offered up that vulnerable part of her. He didn't take her confidence in him lightly…even if he suspected that she was possibly regretting confiding in him.

That's probably why she shut down right after.

And why she was avoiding him now.

I don't want to talk about it, please, she'd requested. It was the sorrow radiating from her that had compelled him to leave well enough alone. She didn't want to discuss the very sad personal thing that happened to her, that was fine by him. He was totally unbothered. Completely. *Entirely.*

At least that was what he had kept repeating to himself unsuccessfully.

Because no matter how he fought it Lulu claimed a good portion of his thoughts lately. And Alwan might have had a smoother time of forgetting what had happened with her had his mother not reminded him of Lulu's absence at yet another one of their wedding planning get-togethers.

"Where is Luula?"

They were sitting at the dining table with his

laptop opened between them and a plethora of different-colored and -sized card stock spread out over almost every inch of the tabletop. A self-professed DIY queen, his mother insisted on them making the save-the-dates for the wedding from scratch. It all just sounded like a lot more work for nuptials that weren't really even going to happen—not that he'd told his mother that. Instead, he'd just attempted to talk her out of her plan. But it had been like trying to get blood out of stone. She was adamant to do it her way and persuade him into lending a hand.

And she'd succeeded, no surprise there.

Though if he *had* refused her, then he'd have been spared his mother's version of a third degree now.

Biting back a sigh, Alwan stared at his laptop and said, "She's busy…again."

It was the same excuse from the day before, and any hope he had that his mother wouldn't notice was dashed when she clucked her tongue loudly at him.

She didn't need to say a word. He heard her suspicion-laced disapproval loud and clear.

Obviously, his mother thought *he* was the reason for Lulu's no-show streak. And he couldn't fault her, because he was starting to believe that too.

Not only that, with all this radio silence on Lulu's end, Alwan had begun secretly worrying she wanted out of their deal. It wasn't a far stretch to believe that she'd changed her mind. He'd promised her a no-strings-attached arrangement, and now that it had gotten more personal than they'd planned, she might have decided to end it.

Despite understanding if Lulu had come to that decision, Alwan still scowled at the possibility. He couldn't recall the last time he'd felt so utterly exhausted and drained on every level and all because of someone else.

It was Hashim, a little voice chimed. His brother was the last person who had made him feel remotely close to what he was feeling now with Lulu. And though it was different, it felt too similar for his comfort.

So, Alwan told himself the only reason he cared was that he couldn't have Lulu backing out of the engagement now. Not when his legal practice was on the line, and not when the shock of the truth would probably destroy the look of bliss on his mother's face as they decorated the save-the-dates together by hand.

Although he and Lulu couldn't avoid the hurt that would inevitably follow when they announced the end of their engagement and wedding plans, they'd already decided how to gently let their families down when the time came.

Four months from now.

Until then she was his fiancée.

Mine.

The possessive claim startled him.

Whoa. Where did that *come from?*

Baffled to his core by that dangerous thought, Alwan hardened his jaw, his body tensing all over from the need to leave his parents' home and go clear his head someplace private. Because under *no* circumstances could he think of Lulu like that again.

She wasn't his.

She'd never be.

And that was how they both liked it.

Liar, the one word curled through his mind like black smoke warning of trouble.

He gritted his teeth and clenched his fists, one around his computer mouse and the other—

"Alwan!"

He startled and looked from his mother's deeply disapproving glare down to the card stock trapped in one of his hands. Loosening his fingers, he tried to smooth out the creases to no avail.

"Sorry," he mumbled, offering her a sheepish smile.

"Something's on your mind." She held up a hand, the irritation gone and stark concern for him creasing her brow. "And please don't say that you're fine. You always say that, and it always means the opposite. Does this have to do with Luula? Is it why she isn't here?"

The lie on his tongue evaporated at the sound of Lulu's name. Tightening his lips, he bowed his head, knowing that if he looked his mother in the eye he'd divulge far more than he wanted to her.

Taking his silence as an affirmative, he heard his mother's deep sigh.

"Whatever you've done—"

"I haven't done anything though," he groused, peeking up at her and grimacing when her glare quickly had him lowering his head again in deference.

"Then why are you sitting here with me, looking so miserable *and* ruining my card stock? Now, do you want my advice or not?"

Alwan knew that she'd be giving it whether he agreed to it or not, so he just nodded.

"Go to her. Talk. Apologize, if you have to, but don't sit here and do nothing. I know you care for her," she said with a pointed look that cautioned him about arguing with her.

Besides, he'd be lying if he didn't want any excuse to see Lulu.

"What about all of this?"

Smiling brightly, his mother stood, gathered the save-the-dates and slid them into his laptop bag. "Think of it as a good excuse to go see her."

Thirty minutes later he showed up at Lulu's

childhood home. He hadn't told her he was coming over, uncertain whether his visit would be welcome.

Gripping the strap of his laptop bag, he rang the doorbell and anxiously smoothed a hand over his beard and down his knit sweater. While he waited for an answer, Alwan's gaze swept the unassuming but peaceful neighborhood, a warm smile lifting his cheeks at the memories he had of being there. Although he and Lulu were far from friends, their parents would often visit each other and he'd always liked hanging out with her younger brother, Liban.

This was the first time he was there to see Lulu.

But it was her younger sister, Ladna, who opened the front door.

"She's upstairs," she said to him after a quick, friendly greeting and inviting him in. "She hasn't been feeling well today and hasn't left her bedroom all that much."

He froze, one foot inside, the other on the threshold. He could hear Ladna call his name a couple times, but all that went through his mind was, *Lulu's sick. She's sick and I've been upset with her.* Picturing her lying in bed, delirious from pain and running a fever weakened his knees and unleashed a wave of nausea in him. *Ya Ilahi.* Alwan didn't know how he was still standing under the tremendous weight of guilt threatening to flatten him.

But he remained on his feet, and stepping inside now, barely acknowledged the concerned look on Ladna's face as he hurriedly set down his laptop bag and slipped off his shoes.

Without saying another word, he bounded up the staircase, two steps at a time.

Behind him he heard Ladna calling his name again.

He didn't need her help finding Lulu's room—there was only one with the door closed—and he knocked briskly.

"Luula, open up. It's me," he said, his hands squeezing the doorframe, his eyes lasered on the door as if he could see through the white-painted wood into her room. "Lu—"

The doorknob twisted and the door pulled open wide.

Wearing her pajamas, Lulu stepped back from the doorway, her hands clutching the fleece throw wrapped around her shoulders and her hair covered by a silk cap. She had no makeup on, and her feet were shod in fuzzy slippers with adorable cat ears. *Yet she's still beautiful.*

A vision of her like that in his home flashed through his mind.

"Why are you here?" she asked and snapped him back to focus.

Pushing out the image, Alwan lowered his hands off the doorframe and walked in, noticing that she slid back another couple steps as he did so. His heart twisted in his chest, but he kept the hurt off his face and out of his voice as he looked her over.

"Ladna told me you weren't feeling too hot. I was… I just wanted to check in on you."

Lulu rolled her eyes and sighed. "She shouldn't have worried you. I'm fine. Or I will be, after I take a nap."

A low yowl sounded from behind her. Alwan looked around her to where her cat watched him with those eerily bright blue eyes from the foot of her bed.

Her bed.

The rumpled bedsheets and distinct head print on her pillow fueled a different kind of fantasy, and it was one that had his body's core temperature running hotter. Blushing, Alwan backed out and stammered, "I—I'll just leave you to it, then. Hope you feel better. Have a good nap." And before he embarrassed himself further, he spun on his heels and sped away as fast as he arrived.

After telling him she'd be sleeping, Lulu didn't know what she expected Alwan to do other than to leave.

But his abrupt departure had her tiptoeing out

into the hallway and listening in on his conversation with Ladna.

"I'm worried about her," her sister was saying.

"I am too," Alwan said.

Breathing slowly through her nose, Lulu rested her head on the wall, regretting that she'd eavesdropped on them. Because now their concern for her wrenched at her heart and almost made her go downstairs and reassure them she was all right.

But that would be a lie.

Lulu heard the front door close behind them, and as the silence of the house closed in, she wrapped her throw tighter around herself and shuffled in her fuzzy slippers back to her bedroom.

"Don't worry," she told Blue when he lifted his head and looked past her with a meow, like he'd expected Alwan to trail in behind her. Flopping down beside him on the bed, she rubbed between his ears. "He's not coming, if that's who you're looking for. He just left and I don't think he's coming back anytime soon."

Seeing Alwan at her home had shocked her.

Caught her off guard.

Particularly when he'd looked and sounded genuinely sincere about checking on her health.

"He wasn't really worried. He couldn't be," she said to Blue. "He's probably just worried I'd be too ill to parade around and play pretend couple with him. That's got to be it." But even as she spoke, Lulu wasn't fully convinced it was that black-and-white, that utterly clear-cut. It'd help if a part of her hadn't felt all warm and fuzzy when she fantasized about why Alwan might have visited. Had he really stopped by on a wellness check? Why would he do that?

Because maybe he cares what happens to me... Is that so hard to believe?

She didn't know what to think anymore. Her temples began to drum the now-familiar beat of a brewing headache, her lower body squeezing with the stirrings of pain again too. Popping a couple painkillers, she lay back down with the still-warm heating pad pressed below her stomach and smiled at Blue as he took his cue and moved out of the way to curl near her feet.

She closed her eyes and just before sleep overwhelmed her consciousness, Lulu's last thought was of Alwan.

When she awoke, it was exactly an hour later.

Lulu sat up, stretched and yawned, sniffing the air and rubbing her grumbling stomach. The pain medication had done its work, and coupled with the nap, she was feeling better. But now she had her hunger to solve. The mouthwatering scent wafting through from downstairs had her salivating.

Licking her lips, she shrugged at Blue as he hopped off the bed and trailed to the door, clearly enticed by the same delightful culinary aroma. "I guess Ladna's back." She knew it couldn't be her mom and dad; they had been so busy flitting about with Alwan's parents and wedding planning, they hadn't had as much focus on their business and were now playing catch-up with the tasks that had piled up.

Stuffing away the guilt to sulk over later, Lulu grabbed her fluffy bathrobe off the back of her computer chair and strolled out into the hall.

She and Blue followed the delicious scent down the staircase, past the small entrance hall through the open living and dining area, and into the kitchen beyond—where Lulu came to an abrupt halt.

Because rather than finding her sister cooking, Alwan was standing there stirring a pot on the stovetop.

She almost rubbed her eyes in disbelief. "Alwan?"

"Oh, good. You're awake." Casting a smile over his shoulder, he opened the cupboards above the counter and pulled down two bowls. "Your timing is perfect because the chicken soup's ready."

Lulu didn't know what was more shocking. That he was responsible for the delectable smell wafting through the whole house, or that he knew the kitchen well enough to know where her parents stashed their china. Not that any of that explained why he hadn't left like she'd assumed he had.

"What are you doing here?" It wasn't the first time that day she'd asked him that, but this time Lulu struggled for a reason to explain his presence. "And why are you wearing my mom's apron?"

Facing her, Alwan swept a hand down the heart-shaped top half of the frilly laced apron. "Are you saying it doesn't suit me? Because I really thought this sunny yellow brought out my eyes."

He grinned when she folded her arms and huffed.

"Okay, not in the mood for jokes, I see. I'm here because Ladna suggested I should stay and keep an eye on you while she was out."

"I bet she did," Lulu grumbled, making a note to have a chat with her meddlesome younger sister.

"Don't be too harsh on her. She's just worried about you. Actually, we both are." Brows creased now and his smile dimmed, Alwan moved a step closer.

Still at her feet, Blue growled.

Shooting a nervous glance down at her snarling cat, he stopped.

"Why don't we sit down and have the soup before it gets cold?" he suggested, already spinning back to the pot on the stovetop. Acting like this homey scene that was playing out was the most normal thing ever, he stirred the chicken soup with a ladle, waving his hand over the curling steam and sighed. "Smells like it's ready. Want a bowl?"

Stunned by how all of this was unfolding, Lulu bobbed her head slowly and watched him place two bowls of soup onto one of her mother's silver serving trays.

Switching off the stovetop, he placed a lid on the pot and then hauling the tray up carefully, walked toward the dining table, but not before slinging her a sunny smile. "Food always tastes better sitting down. At least that's what my mom says."

Never had Lulu been more nonplussed in her life.

First, he dropped in for an unplanned visit. Then he cooked for her. *And now?* Now he was acting like a consummate gentleman.

Lulu looked down to Blue, who meowed up at her and lashed his puffed-up tail. Dropping to her haunches, she gave his back and tail a couple long strokes and whispered, "Should we trust him?" Her stomach gave a low answering rumble, reminding her that her hunger was at stake.

"On second thought, I guess we have no choice," Lulu said, and Blue chirruped back with what she presumed was a warning to be cautious.

Though the dining table seated six, Alwan arranged two place mats beside each other. Not wanting to be rude, Lulu pulled out the chair by him and sat down. But she'd barely picked up the spoon by her bowl before Alwan sprang back up.

"Oops, forgot something. Where's your cat food?"

Confused, Lulu said, "In the pantry. Why?"

"I fed you. It's only fair that I feed the little beast too," he said, his charming grin drying up any urge she had to scold him for calling her cat a "beast."

Yowling, Blue kept a far distance from Alwan, but he didn't hesitate to creep up to his food bowl and dig into his favorite wet cat food the second Alwan stepped back.

"Maybe I was wrong about you, Beast?" Alwan stroked Blueberry's back but tugged his hand out of harm's way when her cat lifted his head and bared his fangs at him. "Or not…"

Lulu sucked in her lips to stifle her laughter, managing to suppress any trace of humor by the time Alwan rejoined her at the table. Feeling his warmth beside her again had her wanting to squirm, and needing something to do, Lulu feigned an inordinate interest in the soup before her.

But she paused with the spoon hovering in front of her mouth when she felt Alwan's unrelenting stare.

"This isn't poisoned, is it?"

His only response was a deep, sexy chuckle, but she took it as a positive sign when he dove into his own bowl.

They ate in silence for a while, but once their bowls were cleared, Alwan leaned closer to her, his features lined with anxiety. "Was it good?"

"I finished it, didn't I?"

"Good," he said murmured, exhaling and flashing her a relaxed smile. "I'm glad. I wasn't sure if chicken soup was the right way to go, but I assumed since you weren't feeling well, it might help. And hopefully it has." He rushed out the last part, his face tensing up again.

My opinion really matters to him. That knowledge had Lulu's heart fluttering just a bit faster. "It's only my period, Alwan. It's not that serious."

He rubbed a hand over his beard, what she now recognized was his nervous little tell. "Oh. Was the soup a bad choice, then?"

"No, it was a good choice. Thank you," she said, knowing he was blushing by the way he smiled shyly and ducked his head.

Again, it struck Lulu that her gratitude affected him so strongly. She'd never have believed it would, but she couldn't deny it either now that she could see it for herself. Of all the people she'd have thought would care about what she thought and how she felt, Alwan would be her last guess. He'd always come off as self-centered to her, so completely absorbed in his own world—it was hard to talk to him without his ego taking up breathing space. Sometimes, it'd even felt as if he'd done it on purpose. *Like he hadn't wanted anyone to get close.*

Lulu studied him while he had his head lowered, intrigued by who he'd turned out to be these last few weeks as her fake fiancé.

He was nothing like the bratty boy she'd thought he was once. Nothing like the man she'd written him off to be.

Whoever he was now had earned a level of trust from her that most people in her life didn't have. Not even her family. Because aside from her doctor, Alwan was one of only two people in the world who knew about her miscarriage.

The other person being her ex-husband.

There was no logic behind telling Alwan. No explanation as to why she'd done what she had, only that it had felt *right* sharing her loss with him.

That same feeling took hold of her now, and

before she knew it, Lulu cleared her throat softly to grab his attention.

Alwan lifted his head.

"I didn't really expect you to still be here. I… haven't *exactly* been holding up my end of our contractual relationship lately, and, uh, well, I wouldn't be surprised if you wanted to back out of this—"

"That won't happen, ever."

Lulu pulled in a sharp breath at the vehement glint in Alwan's narrowed eyes and the gravel now roughening his deep voice.

"Unfortunately, you're stuck with me," he said, his stare intensifying with every one of her heartbeats. "At least until the end. Until we've both decided we're done."

A dragging beat of silence passed, and then he asked, "Are we done, Luula?"

Eyes wide and lips parted, she shook her head slowly.

"Good. Will you help me clear the table, then?"

Still having trouble finding her voice, Lulu gave him a nod and trailed him into the kitchen. They cleaned up quietly for the most part, but near the end, he looked over at her.

"You are feeling better, right?"

"I am." Wiping down the counter, Lulu hazarded a peek at him. "Just so you know, you don't have to be worried about me. None of this pain I'm going through is new."

"I figured it couldn't be. You seemed to be able to handle it at the restaurant," he reminded her.

"Yeah, I've gotten better at coping. Only because for as long as I remember, my body's been this way, so I'm pretty used to it. My official diagnosis is lean PCOS. The awful cramps, the bloating, nausea, dizziness, headaches and mood swings." Lulu stopped wiping, her fingers digging into the cloth in her grasp, her eyes glued to the now spotless counter. "The only part I've never been able to handle is the infertility issues…and the higher risk of miscarriage."

She heard Alwan's deep inhale right before he said, "We don't have to talk about this."

Stung that it felt like he was shutting her down, Lulu looked up, her brows knitted and a frown pulling down her mouth. "Is this about what happened in your car a few days ago? Because if you're upset—"

"God, no." Alwan pushed off the counter he'd been leaning on, walked over to her and, pulling the cleaning cloth fisted in her grasp free, tossed it aside. Then took her hand. Kneading her fingers softly with his, he gazed down into her eyes and said, "If you want to talk about it, then I'm all ears. But don't feel like you owe it to me. The only thing that happened in the car was that you were protecting yourself, as you should. Don't *ever* apologize for that. Not ever."

Lulu blinked, the heat creeping from the back of her eyes summoning tears.

He squeezed her hand, and she quietly gripped him back.

"I—I want to talk about it."

"Okay," he said and then stood there silently and patiently waiting for her to speak her mind.

It took her a moment, but she stoppered the waterworks and successfully cleared most of the hoarseness from her voice. "Losing the baby was always a strong possibility. But Mohamed and I, we still wanted to try."

"Mohamed's your ex, right?"

She nodded, quietly clocking how Alwan's dark eyes narrowed, his strong jaw stiffened and he jerked his head in understanding.

"We both knew that it wouldn't be easy or fast, and that we'd need to exercise a lot of patience. IUI and IVF weren't also options, not with our finances. And the publicly funded waitlist would've had us waiting years before getting a chance. Mohamed was hopeful we wouldn't need to go those routes, and I… I let his hope carry us both away.

"We waited three years and a handful of chemical pregnancies before, finally, it happened. A positive. A real one this time.

"We were both so happy," she said, looking down to where Alwan held her, his thumb drawing lazy circles on her hand, his fingers gently squeezing now and again.

"I let Mohamed talk me into shopping for the baby. Toys, clothes, we even started planning how to tell everyone. We were only seven weeks along. We should've known not to get carried away. Should've known to dial it down. It all just felt too good to be true. Too good to be *real.*

"A few days later, we lost the baby. And a little more than a month after that, Mohamed and I decided to file for our divorce."

"Luula," Alwan rasped her name, his fingers gripping hers. "I know no words in the world can convey my condolences, but I am sorry. Sorry that you couldn't be the mother you'd dreamed to be. Sorry that you had to endure a pain no one should go through. Sorry that you couldn't hold your child in your arms.

"I wish I could say I was sorry that your relationship ended, but no man—*no* life partner worthy of that title—would've let you go, not then, not when you needed support the most. I'm glad this Mohamed walked off when he did. He didn't deserve you from the start." Alwan interlaced their fingers and stared down at her as fiercely and passionately as he stated his thoughts.

Lulu pushed the numbness back from taking

complete hold of her and looked up at him with a weary smile.

"It's not his fault. It was just…too much for him to handle. I can't blame him for that."

Scowling, Alwan still appeared unconvinced.

As touched as she was that he was incensed on her behalf, she knew that it wouldn't change what had happened. And she hadn't told him any of this just to drag him down into the same dark headspace she'd felt trapped in for so long. It wasn't a place she would've wished on anyone, least of all him.

Lulu pressed the hand he wasn't holding to his warm, solid chest.

Alwan immediately lifted his free hand and clasped hers over his heart.

"Does your family know about your loss?"

She shook her head. "I don't want to worry them…"

Alwan's fingers massaged the back of her hand soothingly.

They didn't speak, just held on to each other for what felt like forever. If it weren't for Blue meowing loudly at their feet and redirecting their attention, Lulu didn't know if they would have moved apart anytime soon. She'd been too comfortable letting Alwan hold her—far too relaxed in touching him right back.

Don't confuse his kindness with something else.

Heeding her own warning, Lulu drew back. Alwan let her go.

"I should probably head back upstairs and rest," she said.

"Are you feeling unwell again?" he asked, his expression flipping to concern in the blink of an eye.

"I'm fine, I promise. Just a little sleepy. Nothing a nap won't cure."

"If you're sure…"

"I am," she said, flashing him a quick smile.

"Okay then, I'll take that as my cue to get out of your way now. And before I forget, here." He pulled her family's house key from his pocket and passed it to her. Seeing her questioning look, he explained, "Ladna gave me her spare, and I went grocery shopping for the ingredients to the soup. I let myself back in with it."

Somehow that knowledge only tugged at her heartstrings more… *If that's even possible.*

"I'll walk you out."

"Sure," he agreed, turning and heading for the front door.

At the entrance, he stopped suddenly and grabbed a slim messenger bag that was tucked between the coatrack and the shoe stand. "I almost forgot. My mom wanted you to have these." Opening the bag, he pulled out a small stack of decorative, delicate-looking cards. A cursory look told Lulu they were save-the-dates. As odd as it was to see her and Alwan's full names on the card, announcing a wedding they both knew would never happen, she had to admit that the cards were uniquely beautiful.

"These are really pretty."

Alwan smirked. "My mom will love hearing that because we made them."

"Sorry, *you* helped make these?" Lulu couldn't believe it. First he cooked, and now this. She wasn't used to complimenting him, figuring his ego never needed more stroking, but even she had to admit that she was in awe of his hidden skills.

"I'm a man of many talents," he preened.

She sighed and shook her head, but she struggled not to smile when Alwan laughed.

"So, take a look at the cards whenever you're ready and let us know what you think." He pulled his shoes on and backed up to the front door, his hand grasping the door handle. "Other than that, uh, I hope you feel better soon. So, um, bye." He gave her a little awkward wave, his smile bordering on bashful as he opened the door and walked out onto the porch.

"Alwan?" Lulu called after him just as he cleared the last step down the porch.

"Yeah?" he asked, lifting his hand to shield his squinting eyes from the sun and looking back up at her.

"Thanks for visiting. It was surprisingly nice."

"Surprisingly?" he laughed and lowered his hand.

Laughing too, she said, "Maybe we can meet up tomorrow and I can give you my thoughts on the cards."

"I'd like that."

Closing the door, and still smiling after their exchange, Lulu turned and looked down to where Blue was peering up at her curiously.

"Don't judge me. He did feed us both, so he can't be that bad, right?"

Meowing, Blue stalked over to her and rubbed against her leg.

Picking up her attention-seeking cat, Lulu carried him upstairs, back to their bedroom where she dropped him gently onto the unmade bed. Purring his satisfaction, Blue kneaded the bedsheets, settling himself down and looking at her as if wondering why she hadn't joined him yet.

Only there was one thing she wanted to do before lying down.

Lowering to her knees, she lifted up the bed skirt and, searching in the darkness under her bed, found what she was looking for.

The small suitcase wasn't anything special on the outside.

But it was what was inside that mattered to her.

Placing her hands atop it, Lulu pulled a deep breath in and out before she pinched the zipper and opened the luggage slowly. Her eyes stung as she pushed back the lid and stared down at the brand-new tiny clothes inside. There were even a couple toys, their packaging undisturbed. She counted to ten before her vision blurred and her hands groped at the lid to close the suitcase.

Pushing it back where she'd pulled it from, she climbed onto her bed and lay down, sniffling quietly.

Blue's wet nose brushed her cheek, his whiskers tickling her.

"It's all right," she said, tucking him beside her and petting him.

And it was. Those hadn't been empty words. She *did* feel better given what she'd just bravely done. Since packing those clothes and toys away a little more than a year ago, Lulu hadn't looked at them again.

But now, not only had she managed to do that, she wasn't spiraling into that awful darkness that had once taken hold of her life right after her loss. And though Lulu wouldn't attribute it to her conversation with Alwan completely, she had a feeling that it played a big role. Talking to him had been far more therapeutic than she could have ever imagined.

He really isn't so bad after all.

More than that, Lulu had to admit she was taking a strong liking to Alwan with every day that passed.

CHAPTER SEVEN

FOR A BIG CITY, Toronto had green spaces spread throughout the metropolis, and Lulu was immensely grateful for it now as she dropped onto her back and sprawled out her limbs on the picnic blanket beside Blueberry.

Her persnickety cat kneaded the spot beside her before settling his rump down and yawning.

She might have joined Blue in taking a nap if they weren't in the heart of busy High Park. Even if the constant foot traffic didn't keep her awake, or the possibility of being robbed, the knowledge that Alwan would be arriving any moment left her too wired to do anything else but wait out the time until he showed up.

It had been a little over a month since he'd stopped by her home to check in on her and ended up making soup for her. *Oh, and feeding Blue.* She couldn't forget that. All of it had been so uncharacteristic. So unlike what she'd expected him to do. His thoughtfulness was at odds with the vanity he'd always shown her.

In fact, Lulu was beginning to wonder if she'd even really *known* him at all.

Because over the past month he'd ramped up his generosity. Scheduling their meetings around her lunch breaks from work rather than his, letting her choose the places where they'd meet up and even treating her regularly to her favorite flavored iced latte. She didn't know what to make of his small shows of kindness. Was he being nice for some ulterior motive, or was it something else?

Something like how he feels sorry for you because of you-know-what...

Pressing her palms over her tightening chest, Lulu shut her eyes and breathed out deeply. She'd accepted that it was possible Alwan was handling her delicately now after everything she had shared with him. Overcompensating with his kindhearted acts because he didn't know what else to do. And if that was the case, she couldn't fault him for simply being considerate. It wasn't as if he'd signed up to be her therapist.

Just my fake fiancé, she thought dryly.

Opening her eyes, Lulu sighed long and deep, feeling the stony weight of it reverberate through her bones. She wanted to regret telling him all that she had, but just like being unable to be irritated with his overfriendliness, she couldn't find it in herself to do that. Because regardless of whether he felt sorry for her or not, Lulu felt better having confided in Alwan about losing her baby and how that led to her divorce. The emotional burden of carrying that baggage around wasn't so hefty now.

Which brought her to this point: as fake as their relationship was, it didn't lessen the very real comfort he'd given her by just listening.

For that, she owed him.

And not liking the weight of that debt, Lulu had devised a way to settle the score.

She pulled out her phone and searched his name. Just like all the other times she'd done this over the last several days, Lulu didn't have to scroll far to find the viral video of Alwan being assaulted by his former client. She'd watched the long clip several times, even seen shortened versions specifically focusing on the exact moment Alwan was hit in the chest by an array of lobbed pastries to the tune of funny circus music and laugh tracks.

Though he hadn't spoken too much about it, and had even acted like it hadn't bothered him, this video was what had inspired him to seek her out.

It was what started all of this for them both.

So, it couldn't be easy for Alwan to accept its existence. But now that he was on this path to a new venture, she presumed that he'd have to want closure, and to do that he'd have to talk about it.

That was where Lulu was hoping to return the favor.

This is how I can help him the way he helped me.

She paused the video on a clear frame of Alwan's shocked face just after he'd been attacked, and just stared and stared at him, her heart squeezing in sympathy and her thoughts carrying her away.

That was how she missed Alwan's arrival until his smooth, deep voice came out of nowhere.

"What are you looking at?"

She yelped, quickly shut off her phone, snapped upright to a seated position and whipped her head over to where he stood behind her. He had his shoulder propped against the large oak tree that she'd placed her outdoor blanket beneath, his laptop bag slung over the other shoulder, and he held a drink tray containing two cups.

Ready to defend her, Blue sprang to his paws, his tail bushy, back arched and fangs bared.

"Whoa, hey, I come in peace." Alwan pushed off the tree and despite his adorable grin, he eyed a hissing Blue warily. "Should I be worried he's going to attack?"

"Blue wouldn't hurt a soul, but it would serve you right if he did with the way you're sneaking around and jump-scaring us like that," Lulu said with a sniff, gathering her cat into her arms just in case she was wrong this one time.

He laughed. "You can't call it *sneaking* if you weren't paying attention to your surroundings. Now, what were you staring at on your phone that had you so interested you didn't hear me coming up behind you?"

"Nothing," Lulu squeaked, blushing. She wasn't about to confess that she'd been snooping on him online. *Nuh-uh. No way.*

"Really? It didn't look like nothing. But, okay, keep your secrets." His smile unbudging, he shrugged and passed her one of the drinks from the tray.

Lulu bundled Blue into one arm, accepted her iced coffee from him and murmured her gratitude. She drank a big gulp and sighed happily, the cold caffeine jolt already working its magic on her frayed nerves after Alwan nearly caught her spying on him.

"I'll take that as a sign I didn't mess up your order," he said, enjoying a sip from his own cup before he sat down beside her on the blanket, his thigh brushing up against hers. The scent of him, all toasted warmth and spiced earth, enveloped her and restoked the heat simmering under her skin. *Well, there goes my composure.* And so much for the coffee icing the fluttery feelings Alwan inspired in her more and more of late.

"So, what's up?" Lulu asked, sounding a little pitchy from her nerves. It was just that they weren't supposed to be meeting this early today. Instead, they'd had plans to see each other in the evening at his parents' home, where apparently his mother had some traditional Sudanese thobes she'd wanted Lulu to choose from for the nikah ceremony.

Not that a nikah would be happening. But they had pretenses to keep up, so Lulu had no choice but to show up.

None of that explained why Alwan had called to see her.

And it wasn't helping calm her when he scrubbed a hand over his bearded jaw and slung her an apologetic smile.

"Have I told you how much I appreciated you helping me find an office? Because I did, *and* I'm going to need your help again," he said.

"With?"

"A dinner."

Recalling how tasty his soup had been and how comfortable he'd appeared working in her parents' kitchen, Lulu frowned and tipped her head to the side. "You want me to help you make dinner?"

"Well, yes, I wouldn't mind the extra hands if

you're offering. But that's not it. Do you remember how I told you that I'm trying to tap into my parents' network of contacts? They have friends and acquaintances within their business circles who could be potential clients for my practice."

Lulu nodded. "I haven't forgotten. It's the whole reason why *this*—" she gestured between them "—is even a thing."

"You mean you don't *actually* want to marry me?" Alwan touched a hand to his chest, his gorgeous features twisting into mock hurt. "Really hurting a guy here, Lu."

She blushed at the easy, affectionate way he'd used her nickname. It rolled off his tongue so naturally and softened her heart for him in a way it shouldn't have, but did anyway. Her body suddenly warmer, she pretended to be occupied trying to keep Blue away from sniffing curiously at her iced coffee. Juggling her cat and coffee, she asked, "What's dinner got to do with anything?"

"One of my parents' acquaintances reached out after they introduced us. He's the former Crown counsel for the Toronto Region, and now runs an internationally successful biotech start-up."

"Sounds like a man who should have a well-heeled litigator on retainer."

Alwan's twinkling eyes and laughter heated her up faster than any hot mid-June afternoon could ever. "You're on my wavelength. This dinner is my chance at pitching him, so everything has to be perfect."

"And when is this perfect dinner happening?"

"A few weeks from now. Though he's from the city and has a home here, he travels a lot for his business and is only going to be stopping by the city for a day or two. Only problem is that my one shot to meet with him is on the evening of Canada Day." He gave her a grimace before rushing to add, "I'll understand if you've already made plans to celebrate with your family or just want the day off to relax. It's not like our contract stipulates that I take up your holidays too. I'll just tell him that something came up and you couldn't make dinner because of it."

"He knows about me?"

"My parents told him about the engagement."

"Oh, of course," Lulu said, not certain why she was so disappointed by that news, or even why she'd leaped to the conclusion that Alwan had cared enough to mention her to this wealthy businessman he was trying to bag as a client. Smiling off the awkward pause, she asked, "Are your mom and dad going to join us?"

"No, the restaurant is open on Canada Day and it's one of their busiest times of the year. But my mom has offered to help me cook." He cocked his head to her with a smirk. "Also, did I just hear you say 'us'?"

"You did."

Lulu bit her lip to stifle laughter when Alwan pumped his fist and hooted his exuberance. A couple runners jogging past tossed them amused looks.

"People are staring at us," she observed, the laugh she was trying to hold in sparkling out. "Are you really that happy that I'm coming?"

"Of course I am! Listen, I didn't say this earlier because, well, my ego."

She snorted and he grinned.

"*But* now that you've said you're going to come through, I'll be honest and say that I'm a little nervous. Okay, fine, *a lot* nervous, but it'll feel good having someone else with me. You know, in case I choke or anything. Not that I mean I'll choke on dinner, hopefully. But you know—"

"Alwan?"

"Yeah?"

"You're rambling," she said with a kind smile at his obvious anxiety over this important business meeting. "It'll go smoothly, with or without me."

"For sure," he said with a nervous-sounding chuckle and a tug at his collar. "Gotta think positively, right? Right. Anyways, we're good for dinner on Canada Day at my place?"

Lulu was mid-sip her coffee and nearly spat it out in her hurry to blurt, "Your place?"

"Is that a problem?"

Yes!

"N-no, it's just, I thought it would be at your parents' home."

"Since they're working, I didn't want to bother them, and besides, I have a perfectly good place of my own to play host. Was that all, or is something else bothering you?"

Yes, the idea of us being together alone, in your home, definitely *bothers me.* Even if they had been alone together before, it was only that every time that happened they ended up getting close emotionally, physically… Then she always was left with these uncomfortable feelings she was clueless what to do about.

But seeing that Alwan was waiting on her, she offered him a reassuring smile. "Nope, I'm all good," she lied, hoping the little squeak at the end didn't give her away.

Appearing not to notice, Alwan beamed at her. "We're solid, then. Dinner at mine."

From an early age, Lulu had always known there was a great disparity in wealth between her family and Alwan's. The gap in financial standing never kept their parents from being close friends though, and so Lulu liked to think of herself as being desensitized to the big houses, flashy cars and designer clothing labels.

And yet, even with all that said, she had a hard time picking her jaw up from where it landed on the gleaming terrazzo flooring when she stepped out of the private elevator and into Alwan's luxury condo for their Canada Day dinner.

Leaving her shoes in the built-in shoe cabinet by the elevator, she walked in slowly, turning her head every which way at the wealth oozing from the walls and furnishings.

The tall, elegantly coved ceilings, beautiful modern light fixtures, expensive-looking artwork and vases would've made this feel like a museum, but there were plenty of touches of greenery, the plant life adding warmth to the space along with several windows bringing in an abundance of sunlight. Lulu gawked at it all, feeling the affluence on a level she'd never anticipated.

It struck her that he lived on a totally different world.

Make that a different galaxy, she thought as she strolled past open French doors into the kitchen and was met by marble floors and walls, a bevy of state-of-the-art appliances, built-in closets and an impressive island with a dark wood base.

"Hey, you made it." Alwan came up behind her, giving her a little startle that was instantly wiped away when he reached for the reusable grocery bags in both her hands.

"Here, let me get those for you," he said.

Though it was only a brief touch, his fingers skimming hers left a tingle with her long after he moved away and began unloading the bags on the island. There was milk, eggs, oil as well as all kinds of fruits and vegetables, seasoning, and finally small bags of rice and flour. Once her parents had learned about the business dinner Alwan was hosting, they'd insisted on chipping in with what they could.

He whistled, his eyes widening in awe. "Whoa. Your mom and dad really went above and beyond. Are you sure they're all right without me paying? Because I'd be more than happy to."

"They know," she said, smiling and walking to the other side of the island across him. "But they were adamant that I bring everything we *could* need for the dinner over here."

Scratching his head, Alwan looked around at the groceries overflowing his island counter. "There is no way we'll be using all of this though."

"I think that's what they were hoping. Knowing them, they're probably worried your fridge is empty, what with the bachelor lifestyle you live. You're just lucky I talked them out of emptying all their shelves and unloading most of their inventory on you."

He laughed before clapping and rubbing his hands together. "Well, then, I guess we better make this the best dinner ever. Don't want to disappoint anyone." Turning to the wall of pantry cabinets, Alwan pulled open one of the cabinet doors and fished out an apron. He passed it over to her and their fingers brushed again, that electric spark dancing through the light contact once more.

"Your dress is too beautiful to ruin," he said with another of his toe-curling, heart-racing smiles.

"What about you?"

He looked down at his plain long-sleeved shirt and light-wash jeans. "I dressed to make a mess. In other words, I should be good until I change for dinner later."

It struck her that it was the first time she'd seen him looking so casual. Usually he was stuck in one of his suits, and though he was dressed down, he still looked good. *Real good.* Had she ever noticed his biceps before? Because she was looking now and with every flex of his muscles, she felt her mouth grow drier, her breath quicken and her body tighten all over with longing.

Giving her head a shake, Lulu realized Alwan had asked her a question.

His small smirk told her that he'd caught her ogling him.

She steeled herself for his taunting, but instead of poking fun, he gestured to the groceries and asked, "Would you help me put some of this away in the fridge? It's not like many places are open today, and I don't want anything spoiling on us. This dinner has to go smoothly if not perfectly."

"Speaking of dinner, what are we making?" She placed her purse down on one of the sleek leather barstools along the island and, tying the apron around her long-sleeved light green maxi dress, looked around and raised an eyebrow at him. "Also are we waiting on your mom?"

"About that. She's not coming anymore." He then explained how the restaurant was even busier than his parents had been prepared for and that because one of their sous-chefs was out sick, his mother had no other recourse but to stay.

Letting it sink in that it was just going to be the two of them, alone, in his home, Lulu tried and failed to quell the little shivery excitement chasing up her spine.

"Is that okay with you? Or do we need to fetch your little beast to guard you from me?"

She placed her hands on her hips. "Blue is neither a beast nor my guard. Anyway, I don't need one. I've got my own claws."

"Feisty. Are you so sure about that?" Setting down a head of lettuce, he stalked around the counter to her, his long fingers trailing along the edge of the island, his dark brown eyes now hooded and fixed on her and his smile a slow, seductive pull of his thick brown lips.

"What are you doing?"

"What do you think that I'm doing?" He stopped before her, drumming his fingers on the granite countertop, that stupid, sexy grin of his making her weak in the knees.

"S-stop teasing me," she stammered and hugged her arms tighter to her chest.

He lowered his head, the space between them growing that much smaller as he whispered, "I'll stop when *you* stop making it so fun. Until then…" Trailing off purposefully, his gaze lowering to her mouth, Alwan moved in—his intent as clear as the day pouring in through the windows.

He's going to kiss me!

Breath hitching at the thought, she shut her eyes instead of shoving him away or running off.

But it wasn't a kiss she experienced.

It was the feel of air brushing along the side of her face. She snapped her eyes open and whirled around once she saw Alwan wasn't standing in front of her any longer. He was strolling toward the fridge, the lettuce back in his hand.

She sputtered quietly, her face heated, her irritation with him warring with her yearning for the kiss he'd denied her. That kiss he clearly never meant to give her, by the way he grinned mischievously at her from the open fridge doors.

"So, fiancée of mine, are you ready to cook with me?"

* * *

"I have to say that was the best dinner I've had in months. The downfall of globe-trotting, I'm afraid. But my compliments to the chef stand." Abdel, the Sudani businessman Alwan had invited into his home, now gestured to Lulu across the table from him.

His smile was as warm as his robust laugh when Lulu quickly corrected him. "As much as I'd love to take credit, Alwan made most of the food. I just contributed the sambusas."

"She's being modest," Alwan said, looking to her and taking in the heightened color in her glowing brown face. *Lovely* didn't begin to capture her attractive qualities to him, but it was a fair attempt. "She helped me out with quite a bit. In fact, I'd go as far to say that this dinner couldn't have happened without her."

Lulu's eyes flashed wide-open, her lips parting with her shock.

"It was a team effort, then," Abdel cut in, the older man nodding.

"A team effort," Alwan echoed before he turned back to regard their guest. "You said it best, sir."

Wagging a thick finger at him, Abdel said, "I thought I warned you not to call me 'sir.' Makes my already old bones feel older."

"With all due respect, sir, my parents would

roll over if they heard me call you by your name. It's either sir, sayidi or ustadh."

Abdel barked another laugh and slapped his hand down over the dining table. "Very well. I'll acquiesce to the honorific, but only for the dessert I know you've both made."

"I'll get it," Lulu said cheerfully, standing before Alwan could. And when he tried to offer a hand to clear the table, she shook her head and gave him a surreptitious look complete with a little jerk of her chin toward Abdel. It dawned on him that she was trying to give him an opportunity to talk shop with the older businessman.

When Lulu left to fetch dessert, Alwan breathed deeply and, feeling braver, leaned forward.

Though threads of white coiled through his short, curly hair, Abdel's gaze was sharp as a blade as he assessed him quietly.

"I see it's come time to discuss business, then," he said, surprising Alwan when he raised a hand. "Before you rush and give me a long-winded speech extoling all your merits, I'd like to ask you something. Are you serious about opening your own legal practice?"

"Of course," Alwan replied quickly, the answer coming to him easily. Right now, right then, he wanted nothing more than for his private practice to take off and do well. It was why he was here. Why Lulu was by his side. Compelled by the thought of her, he flicked a glance over to where she worked in the kitchen. And just one look at her and his heart jolted faster, his cheeks warming up when he turned back to Abdel and found the older man looking back at him with a small knowing smirk.

"And that, right there, is why I'm asking." Abdel nudged his head to the kitchen with a hoarse chuckle. "I recognize that look because I've seen it on my own face whenever I'm near my wife.

"It's no wonder, then, that when I'm asked what I attribute my success to that I always answer with her name. Despite my late work nights, my overly filled schedule and the last-minute meetings interrupting our plans, she remains my main pillar of support even after almost fifty years of marriage. In fact when I told her about this dinner, she wanted to be here, but she's helping our daughter care for our first grandchild.

"Now, the reason I'm telling you this is because you remind me of myself when I was young, enterprising and so sure that I could juggle every aspect of my life smoothly. You're about to be married though, and from what I see, you care for your fiancée very much and she feels the same for you."

Alwan was stunned into silence. Was he

being that obvious about his affection for Lulu? This baffling, bone-deep need to look at her, be around her and soak in all the attention she was willing to give him reading so clearly to everyone else but him.

And was what Abdel said about Lulu true?

Does she care for me too?

Alwan glanced over at her, the urge too strong to ignore or tamp down even as he looked back at Abdel and asked, “Are you saying all this because you’re not interested in working with me?”

The older man shook his head. “What I’m saying is that I want you to seriously consider the sacrifices running your own business will require. Your parents have spoken highly of you… but also of your ambition. From personal experience, I wouldn’t advise it’s the best trait for a marriage.” Abdel paused and looked over to the kitchen and Lulu again. “But in regard to business, I like that your practice, much like my own company’s medical technology, intends to help those who our laws and society don’t always empower. Yes, your parents told me that part too,” he said with a benevolent smile. “Which is why, as a family man myself, I have no doubt that you’ll be an asset and not a liability to me.”

Understanding what he meant, Alwan had to fight not to jump up and shout out from sheer exhilaration. Hoping he looked calm and composed, he accepted Abdel's handshake and pumped the older man's fist.

"I'll still need to hear a full proposal, and bring you in to speak to my executives and board of directors, but I see a promising future partnership for us both." Abdel smiled toward Lulu as she walked over with a tray of smaller plates of basbousa in her hands. Made of ghee, yogurt and shredded coconut among many ingredients, the semolina cake was a favorite in many Middle Eastern and North African countries. It smelled as sweet as it tasted and Alwan wasn't alone in appreciating the traditional dessert.

Abdel rubbed his hands together and beamed happily. "My, I'm being treated like a king today. Fine food. Finer company. Careful, I might not want to leave."

They all shared in laughter.

Despite what he'd said, Abdel did eventually announce his departure, but he didn't leave empty-handed. Lulu persuaded him to take some of the cake they'd made. Seeing how happy her gesture made Abdel had Alwan wanting to hug her for her thoughtfulness. Resisting the instinct to take her in his arms was difficult, especially as it intensified when they were alone in his home again.

"What? Is there something on my face?" she asked when he trailed her from the elevator where they bid Abdel farewell back to the kitchen where she'd already started cleaning up. He'd been leaning against the island, watching her place the rest of the basbousa into a food storage container before walking it to the fridge.

She wiped at her cheeks when he didn't stop staring.

"Alwan, what is it? You're freaking me out."

He shook his head slowly, unsteadily, the need for her squeezing his lungs tight, fisting his throbbing heart and making him run hot and cold and all at once— Blinking out of his daze, he said, "I just…wanted to thank you for helping with everything. But most of all for showing up."

"You don't have to do that. At least for the time being, we're a team, so your wins are mine and vice versa."

Team.

There was that word again. Abdel had used it to describe them as well, and it'd sounded good then. *Just as it sounds good now*, he thought.

"Even so, my gratitude stands." He slid a step closer to her, then another.

She looked up at him, that tantalizing rush of blood just under her cheeks was back and her pouty mouth called to him on a primal level begging to be claimed.

Earlier he'd nearly tossed out all his doubts and kissed her. It would've been a mistake—a big one, he knew that. The kind of error that Alwan wouldn't be able to walk back easily. Not with Lulu, and certainly not with himself. Because kissing her would mean acting on his attraction and letting her know how he felt about her.

And since he shouldn't be feeling *anything* for her, a kiss was completely, totally, beyond forbidden territory.

Yet he still wanted to do it.

A muffled boom from someplace outside ripped away the moment.

"Fireworks," she murmured. "Guess the celebrations are starting."

"Did you want to go up to the terrace?"

Alwan led her upstairs to his private oasis, realizing that they'd been so busy cooking all afternoon and then entertaining through the evening that he hadn't had a chance to give her a full tour of his home yet. He promised himself he would another day, even if a little voice taunted, *Will you even have time for that?* It was true. The clock on their deadline was ticking closer with each day that passed, bringing them nearer to the reality that she'd probably never again have a reason to set foot in his home.

Shaking off the hurt that bloomed with that thought, Alwan smiled over at Lulu as she passed him and twirled in place with her arms stretched out, her delight in his rooftop terrace instantly cheering him up.

"This is where we should've had dinner," she exclaimed. "You have a whole kitchen up here!"

"What can I say? I love a good cookout, and it saves me from making trips up and down the stairs."

Lulu shook her head with a smile. Plopping onto the outdoor sectional sofa, she gently touched her fingertips to the pale yellow petals of the jasmines on a trellis and her gaze wandered up to the fairy lights strung above on the pergola. She gasped a soft, sweet sound, the whites of her eyes clearer in the dusk as the sky lit up with fireworks.

"I get some pretty good views up here." He sat down beside her, resting back on a couple cushions and tucking an arm behind his head as he divided his attention between the display lighting up the night sky and sneaking peeks at her.

For a short while they quietly watched together, but as soon as there was a lull between fireworks, Alwan looked over to her and said, "Abdel wants to work with me. It's not a done deal yet, but he's reassured me that he's strongly interested. Again, I couldn't have done that without you."

"You're giving me too much credit."

"No, don't do that whole humble thing. I was

there, remember? I saw what you did, and you deserve every bit of credit."

Smiling and smoothing her hands over the long skirt of her billowy green dress, Lulu curled her legs up on the sofa and hugged a cushion to her chest. "Fine. But if anything, it was your cooking that sealed the deal. That…what did you call it? Bas-something?"

He chuckled. "Basbousa. It means 'small kiss.'"

"Oh, does it now? That's interesting." Lulu's eyes shifted ever so subtly to his mouth, but Alwan hadn't missed it or the way she lightly bit her lower lip and hummed softly, distractedly.

"A sweet meaning for a sweet dessert… Seems fitting to me."

Still staring at his mouth, Lulu murmured, "Yeah, me too."

Sheer willpower kept him from sliding over the small space between them on the sofa, taking her chin in hand and seeing for himself if she tasted as sweet as she smelled and looked.

The fireworks whooshing up, exploding and crackling overhead saved him from falling victim to temptation again.

And this time when the pyrotechnics took another intermission, Alwan stood to stretch his legs and walked to the edge of the terrace, his back to her now, the city with its carpet of bright lights spread out before him. His attempt to create distance didn't last long though. Her richly floral perfume reached him first, her voice following as she came to stand beside him.

"So, does everyone in your family know how to cook? Or did that gene skip your brother?"

Alwan thought desiring her and fighting his longing was tough, but then he hadn't anticipated that they'd be talking about Hashim. Even on a good day his brother was the last subject he wished to discuss. Lulu had no idea though, and he couldn't exactly tell her why, worried more about what questions she'd ask him then.

Because if she did, Alwan didn't trust himself not to spill his family secrets to her. Just being near Lulu made him want to share more of his life with her than anybody else. But this was one thing that he wasn't prepared to tell her, so he aimed a small smile down at her and gave her what she sought: an answer.

"Genetics didn't really have anything to do with it. The reality was more that we were roped in to help out at the restaurant sometimes, so we just picked up the skills along the way."

"Still, that's sweet. I like that you all share a passion for making food. I guess it's true—a family that cooks together, stays together."

She didn't know how far off the mark she was with that comment. But he masked his grimace behind another forced smile, relieved to see that Lulu wasn't even looking at him any longer.

Resting her hands on the balcony railing, she was gazing ahead at the cityscape from his rooftop, her line of sight as far off as the CN Tower piercing the horizon like a lit-up needle. "I envy my parents and yours. That's what I would've wanted for my children, you know, if my…*circumstances* were different."

His heart pulsed for her, his hand already moving, covering hers on the railing, his fingers squeezing her comfortingly.

A moment later, he said, "I can't speak on your parents, but as for mine, let's just say that it's not as clear-cut."

Lulu turned her head up to him slowly.

Swallowing thickly, Alwan pushed himself to continue now that he'd started down this road. "Sometimes families look perfect on the outside, and that's just it. Assumptions. Perceptions. What they hold up to the world because reality… Reality is a lot less perfect." He gazed out at the city, the buildings and streets and trees all blurring to him. It took him a moment to realize why.

I'm crying.

Blinking fast, he coughed around the knot that formed in his throat, embarrassment heating him up from the inside out. But he couldn't stop now. She'd ask more questions, and that wouldn't make it easier on him. *No, I have to finish this.* Speak his mind and get through this as quick as possible. And hopefully, *just* hopefully it wouldn't be as painful as it felt now.

Alwan unclenched his jaw. "The reality is my…my family isn't so perfect."

"Alwan," Lulu whispered his name.

He wanted to look at her, but he kept his head dead straight, his vision still swimming with unshed tears.

"Hashim… We…"

Ya Rabbi.

This wasn't easy. The only thing helping was the feeling of her hand on his arm, her fingers pressing gently and anchoring his disjointed thoughts.

"The truth is Hashim isn't in Sudan. That was just a lie my parents told because we…we don't know where he is." Closing his eyes, he hurried through the rest. "We haven't known his whereabouts for a long time now. He's out there somewhere, or maybe he isn't anymore. All we know is that he's gone." *And probably never coming back.*

"Oh, I'm so sorry, Alwan."

"I am too," he said gruffly, eyes still closed and stinging from the tears he held back.

"I…don't know what to say."

Alwan understood how she felt. Even after all

these years, it was still a lot for him to take in and accept too.

"Have you and your parents tried to look for him?"

He nodded, his head heavy. "My mom and dad hired private investigators, but any trail Hashim left led nowhere. And when my parents gave up searching, I tried, but my efforts were fruitless too."

"Do you want to talk about it?" Lulu asked, her sweet voice too alluring to ignore.

Opening his eyes, Alwan finally allowed himself to look at her and shook his head.

"Not really, no."

When she turned to him fully, he did the same. She touched his dress shirt, her hand over his slim tie, fingers scraping his buttons as she slid her palm up. The heated trail she left in her wake was a mixture of the same physical longing he felt for her and something else…

Something just as strong but nameless.

Lulu stopped her hand above his throbbing heart and, with a compassionate smile, said, "Then we don't talk about it."

He recalled what Abdel had said, how Alwan cared for Lulu and she for him. At the time he couldn't believe it, but now—*now*—looking down into her kind eyes, he wondered how he'd missed it. Because it was clear, on some level, that she did.

He already knew what he felt for her was a strong attraction and whatever that something else he was having trouble labeling was…

Affection, he thought after a little while, his hand curling atop Lulu's over his chest.

That was what he was feeling and hadn't been able to name but suspected all along.

I... I like her.

CHAPTER EIGHT

"WOW, THE SPACE has really come together."

Lulu made the remark softly to herself as she walked into Alwan's office. It'd been a while since she had last set foot there, and in the couple weeks of her absence, he and his newly hired staff had decorated the interior.

Potted ferns sat in a couple corners, adding spots of rich color to the sterile white walls and gray flooring. They had hung up large, framed, colorful photographs of various Toronto landmarks and brought in bookshelves that warmed the space, not that any of the legal texts sitting on the shelves were her idea of fun reading.

What she liked most though was the handwoven, vibrant Turkish rug filling the empty space at the center of the room. The reception desk sat atop it, the chair currently empty, but its smiling occupant walking toward her from one of the smaller offices.

"Hey, Luula. We weren't expecting you, but it's good to see you nonetheless." Uzoma's sunny grin was, as always, hard to resist. Freshly enrolled in a law practice program, and tech savvy like most early twentysomethings these days, Alwan's new office manager had been a choice hire. "Were you looking for Mr. Eltahir?"

Lulu smiled at the formal deference he was showing his new boss. "I am. Has he stepped out?" She looked over at his office, the glass walls making it easy to see the room was empty.

"He's in a meeting." Uzoma pointed over to the larger of the three offices, the room that Alwan had repurposed into a small conference room.

On arriving, she had noticed the drawn blinds, but hadn't assumed anyone was in there. *Weird.* Frowning, Lulu met Uzoma's curious eyes.

"Is he, um, doing okay?"

"Last I checked he was fine. A little busier than usual though."

Relief swept over her at that news.

"If it's important, I could interrupt," Uzoma offered. "I'm sure he wouldn't mind stepping out a moment for you."

"It can wait," she said just as Alwan's paralegal strolled over to them. Like Uzoma, Jagnoor was fairly young but smart as a whip on paper and fun to be around in person.

Greeting the other woman, Lulu laughed when Jagnoor gasped, "Is that what I think it is?"

She was goggling down at the brown paper bag Lulu was holding.

“It is. I passed the food truck on the way over, and I couldn’t resist.” Lulu placed the bag down on Uzoma’s desk and stepped back, giving Jagnoor the honor of pulling out the boxes.

“I wasn’t sure what everyone would like, so I bought one of each flavor.”

Jagnoor opened a box with a happy little squeal. “You’re now officially my bestie, Lulu.”

Uzoma looked over her shoulder with a bemused laugh. “All this excitement for a cake on a stick?”

“Not just any old cake, but a *cheesecake*.” Jagnoor gripped the end of the stick holding the confection and held it up to him. “Look at that caramel-on-chocolate combo and convince me you aren’t drooling.”

Uzoma shrugged, leaned in and took a bite. “Mmm, okay, all right. I’ll admit it’s pretty good,” he agreed with another laugh.

“Right? And you know what would make it better? Coffee.”

“Let’s grab some, then.” Uzoma turned his bright smile from Jagnoor over to Lulu and extended the invite to join them.

“No, I’m fine, thanks. I’ll just wait here for your boss,” Lulu told them, looking over to the conference room.

They walked out together, chatting and laughing all the way.

She watched them go and already missed the diversion they offered with their humorous company. Because now she was back to worrying and hand-wringing, just as she had on the cab ride over.

It had all started when Alwan's parents had called her at work. They usually never reached out to her and only because it was easier for them to get Alwan to pass along messages. So, feeling a little uneasy, she had phoned them back during her lunch break. Whatever it was had to be serious. Strangely though, all his mother and father wanted to know was whether she and Alwan were free to stop by the restaurant later. When she'd asked if they had plans that Alwan forgot to mention to her, they hurriedly assured her that they only wanted to have dinner with them. They had then asked her to let Alwan know since they couldn't seem to reach him.

Lulu had tried calling him right after with the same result.

Alwan's phone had rung and rung and gone straight to his voicemail.

She'd then tried texting, but with no luck there too.

Before long an hour had passed with no word on his end, her texts and calls still unanswered.

Now concerned for a different reason, Lulu had requested finishing up her work outside her office. "For personal matters," she'd reported to her boss. She'd then hailed a cab and headed straight for Alwan's office building, stopping only for the cheesecake slices she'd brought.

Pacing the reception area, Lulu dropped down onto one of the comfy armchairs across from the conference room. She looked between the closed blinds and the glass door. It would be all too easy to sneak up and peek in on his meeting, but it didn't sit right with her to spy on him. Obviously whatever was being said was private. And given the sensitive nature of his job, it wasn't strange for him to be careful.

Still, it didn't mean she wasn't curious and worried.

Between that and his parents' out-of-the-blue invitation to dinner, her nerves were wound tight and a hair trigger away from exploding on her.

Lulu tapped her foot impatiently, crossing her legs—and then uncrossing them and springing up and pacing the distance between the desk and the small open waiting area. The cool, hushed atmosphere of the office amplified the loud rattling thoughts in her head and the thumping of her heartbeat in her ears. At one point the ducts above her head knocked loudly as the air-conditioning switched on and she startled at the jarring noise.

She did it again when the door to the conference room clicked open and voices filtered into the space, one was new to her, but the other—the other had her heart pitter-pattering. *Alwan.* By now she could recognize his smooth-as-melted-chocolate voice blindfolded.

The man he was talking to had a nervous catch to his speech as he said, "Th-thanks again for seeing me on such short notice. I didn't mean to drop this in your lap all over again, especially after how I reacted last time."

"Say no more, Kyle. It's forgiven and forgotten," Alwan replied with a lighthearted laugh, his tone friendly. "I'll reach out to you with a decision in the next day or so."

Thanking him once more, Alwan's visitor, a pale, dark-haired, bespectacled man stepped out of the conference room with Alwan closely on his heels.

Seeing her the moment they walked out, both men stopped immediately and stared at her.

Alwan spoke up first. "Luula? What are you doing here?"

Feeling her face growing hot from all the attention, she moved closer to him and, smiling at his familiar-looking guest, said, "I just wanted to surprise you."

Alwan looked from her to his visitor and back again, nodding. “Right,” he drawled out the one word, a smile slowly drawing up his lips. “Of course, and what a pleasant surprise it is.” He cleared his throat then. “Kyle, may I introduce you to my lovely and talented fiancée?”

“Brains and beauty,” Kyle said, shaking her hand and pushing his glasses up the bridge of his nose. “I wish you both a happy marriage. Now, I’ll leave you two alone. Thank you once again for squeezing me into your schedule, Alwan.”

Lulu waited a full minute to ensure they were alone, before asking, “Was that the guy from the viral video? The one who…” She mimed a throw.

“That’s him,” he confirmed with an amused smile.

“What was he doing here, and why was he thanking you?”

Alwan nudged his head back to the conference room. “Let me explain in there.”

Lulu walked ahead of him into the room and he closed the door behind them, then whisked open the blinds.

“Kyle was here because he wants me to handle his appeal and try and secure a retrial for his case.”

“And is that why he was thanking you, because you said you’re going to do it?”

“No.” Tipping back his head, Alwan scrubbed

both his hands down over his face and sighed heavily, his dark brows slashing together as his eyes locked on the long conference table before him. “I told him I’d think on it and call with my final decision.”

“After everything he put you through, I’d understand why you wouldn’t.” Lulu pulled out a chair and sat down, sitting up straighter when Alwan sighed again and looked at her.

“That video circulating was, frankly, a nightmare. The public might have been casting their stones at me, but he’s gotten plenty of backlash too. Kyle also has kids, and his family hasn’t exactly been getting the privacy they need.”

“Is that why the blinds were drawn?”

Alwan nodded. “He was uncomfortable. I don’t think he even made eye contact with Uzoma when he walked in and asked to see me.”

“You feel bad for him. That could be a reason to take the case.”

“Or not. I can’t risk getting too emotional this time, not with the practice still being new,” he said and gripped the back of a chair, a helplessness twisting his handsome features. “What should I do, Lu?”

It was like when he’d asked for her opinion choosing his office. Lulu had resisted sharing her thoughts then, and she should now. Because as touched as she was that Alwan trusted her enough to ask her to weigh in on what was clearly a very important decision for him, the fact was he wouldn't do that unless he valued her greatly.

And if he valued her *that* much, then…

Then he probably cares for me too.

Something neither of them should be doing given they had promised not to complicate this unusual arrangement of theirs with feelings. It was easier for them both this way. *Safer even*, Lulu thought.

There wasn't room in her to love anyone again. The pain of losing her baby and then watching her ex-husband pull away from her before their divorce was not an experience she wished to relive. Not that she thought Alwan loved her…

If Lulu had believed that, then she wouldn't have hesitated like she was now and would've walked out of the room right then and there.

And since that wasn't the case she stayed put right where she was and said, "Do you really want my help?"

He nodded quickly, eagerly.

"Okay. Tell me about Kyle first. Clearly his case matters to you, but why?"

Alwan then told Kyle's sad tale, starting with how the man lost his wife to a short battle with cancer, and then how one of their adopted children lived with a severe intellectual disability that required more hands-on support. The legal dispute between Kyle and his late wife's extremely wealthy family happened after his wife's dying will and testament requested that her inheritance from her parents be transferred to Kyle and their kids.

"Kyle and his wife had always relied on that inheritance to be a trust fund for their two children if anything were to happen to them. The worst part is that before lawyers were called and courts visited, when his wife was still alive, Kyle had had a good relationship with his in-laws. They'd even supported the adoption and never treated the children any differently. But now, all of a sudden, they've turned their backs on him. And family—family should be there for each other, no matter what." Alwan's jaw hardened visibly, his lips tightening into a thin, severe line and his brows slashing over his narrowed eyes.

Lulu admitted the story was upsetting, but Alwan's reaction felt…personal.

Like he's thinking about his brother.

Whatever had happened between him and Hashim had been painful enough for it to inspire the raw emotions now darkening his features.

Her heart lurched sharply for him, the ache prompting her to speak up and get his mind off his troubles.

"It sounds like you're invested already," she observed softly. "So, what's holding you back?"

"The fact that Kyle drained the last of his savings on his initial court battles and won't be able to pay any new legal fees anytime soon."

"I know finances and income are crucial for your practice at this stage, but since you've been doing all that volunteer work for that nonprofit anyway, couldn't you also take this on pro bono?"

"I did think of doing that," he said with a small smile, the sight of it promising.

"Then it's not money that's making you hesitate, is it? I watched that video, Alwan, and it would be natural if you were worried about that happening to you again. Most people would, myself included."

"Another viral video happening again is a fear, but the truth is I think I'm more scared of the disappointment."

"Letting down your client?" she asked.

"Yes, but also myself," he said, gritting his teeth and rubbing his hands over his face with a groan. "I just don't want anything to go wrong. With this case, with this business…" He lowered his hands, looked over at her then and left his thought incomplete, making her briefly wonder what else he'd been about to say.

Not wanting to delve into why he was staring at her so intensely and so suddenly, Lulu said, "You should do it, then."

He raised his brows. "Why?"

"Because I think even more than losing this case and disappointing yourself, you're really more worried about not doing anything to help."

"And that's because you know me so well?" he said with a wry lift of his lips.

"No, that's because you traveled thousands of kilometers to ask me to be your fake fiancée, and all because you were driven enough by *this* dream, this business of yours that I know will help people who need their voices and stories heard most."

Alwan clamped his lips together, and though his beard concealed his jawline, Lulu knew it was as sharp and hard as steel right now.

Had she crossed a line, some boundary that she shouldn't have? Before she could ask or even try to remedy whatever mistake she made, he cleared his throat and looked off to the side, almost as though he was embarrassed.

"I don't know what to say. Other than I'm grateful." Turning his head back to her slowly, their eyes met and Alwan smiled, his face far more relaxed and the pink undertone to his light brown cheeks brighter with his shyness as he rasped, "Thank you, Luula."

"Of course," she chirped, blushing now too.

"So, why did you stop by?" Alwan was rolling down the sleeves of his button-up shirt as he asked her.

"Your mom and dad called. They've invited us over to dinner at the restaurant."

Frowning, he pulled his suit jacket off the back of one of the conference chairs. "That's odd. Did they give you a reason why they called you instead of me?"

"Well, apparently they tried calling you, but you weren't picking up your phone."

Alwan genuinely looked surprised as he patted his trouser pockets and then checked inside his suit jacket before he snapped his fingers. "Right. I left it behind in my office. Probably put it on silent too. I've been working out of this room for most of the day between meetings with some of my old clients and with Abdel and his team."

"How's it going with Abdel?"

"Good," he said with a big grin. "His people are sending over the contracts to make it official."

"That's great news!" Lulu didn't want to dampen his spirits but she needed to speak her mind, so she added, "I'm a little worried about what your parents might want. Do you think they know we aren't really…you know, *romantically involved*?"

He was silent for a moment, and then he shook his head. "I highly doubt it. If my parents knew, they wouldn't be sitting on the news without immediately giving me an earful about it. Literally.

As in they'd be pulling on my ear and yelling at me."

"Are you so certain?"

"I mean, I'm hopeful," he chuckled. "But that isn't what you want to hear."

"Not one bit," she said with a sigh and a small tired smile.

"Don't worry. Even if they do know and want to ream us out, we're in this together."

After everything she'd just done to redraw the boundary line between them, Alwan had gone and blurred it again and with only one word. *Together.*

For Lulu's sake, Alwan had put on a brave face as they later drove to his parents' lakefront restaurant.

He knew she was nervous and used every opportunity to remind her that he was right by her side and wasn't going anywhere. When he parked his car, he reassured her again that he would be there with her every step of the way. When they walked up to the building, he held the door open for her and gave her an extra big smile. And when the hostess instructed them to go upstairs, and it was only him and Lulu in the elevator together, Alwan sidled closer to her, brushed the back of his hand against hers and looked down at her.

Without saying a word, he tried to communicate that they would be all right.

Lulu must have gotten his message because she offered him a conciliatory smile right as the elevator pinged and the doors slid open.

"Surprise!"

The loud cheers and sound of confetti poppers had Alwan immediately covering Lulu with an arm, his instinct to protect her riding over his confusion as he assessed the unusual sight before him.

People. Dozens of people were standing in front of the elevator and staring back at him and Lulu. All people he knew. Family, friends, aunties and uncles from both the Somali and Sudani communities, and even neighbors who lived near his parents' home whom Alwan hadn't spoken to in a long while. But there were also faces he didn't recognize; faces he was starting to realize probably belonged to Lulu's friends and extended family.

Lulu squeezed the arm he had thrown in front of her and whispered, "Did we just walk into a party?"

"It seems so."

Before Alwan could answer, someone cried, "Let's get the party started!"

Of course it was Malek. Pushing his way to the front of the crowd, his cousin strode into the elevator and obnoxiously blew a kazoo in Alwan's face. "Come on, you two. As the guests of honor you can't leave everyone hanging." Waving at them to exit the lift, he made some sort of signal that had the music turning on.

As soon as they cleared the lift, Alwan was pulled one way and Lulu the other into embrace after embrace. Everybody was taking a turn congratulating them on their engagement. By the time they were standing together again, it was under a beautiful, intricate balloon arch with his arm wrapped around Lulu's shoulders and a photographer snapping their pictures.

"Stand closer, lovebirds," Malek called out, laughing when his wife, Rima, gave him a censuring look, though even she appeared as amused as everyone else.

After what felt like forever, the photographer signaled for Lulu's parents and sister and his mother and father to join them in the pictures. Then other relatives jumped in and friends after that.

Taking it with stride, Alwan laughed along and smiled with everybody, all while inside his anxiety jangled louder with every second that passed. Because he hadn't had a moment alone with Lulu to gauge how she felt about all of this. Though she flashed pretty smiles for the camera and chatted contentedly enough with their family and friends, he knew better than to take her cheerfulness at face value.

She can't be happy.

It was his fault for not calling back his parents and grilling them until they confessed about the surprise party. He'd have to find a way to make it up to her, starting with a rescue. But it wasn't easy finding an opening.

After taking photos for what felt like a whole hour, they were pulled over to the cake table, where they took more pictures, and then he and Lulu were obliged to make a speech thanking everyone. Hoping that was all of it, Alwan bit back a groan when their well-wishers started making toasts blessing a marriage that he knew wouldn't ever be happening. It was tough sitting through that part, staring into the faces of all these people who cared for them and knowing he and Lulu were lying to them.

But I'm the one that wanted this.

Lulu hadn't approached him with the fake engagement, and she'd only signed up because he had tempted her with the money she had needed for the repairs on her motor home.

Thinking on that only made him feel worse.

And if it wasn't easy for him, it had to be harder for Lulu, especially when some of the blessings mentioned children. Every time that happened, Alwan flicked a concerned look at her, but her beautiful smile and bright eyes gave nothing away.

Biding his time for a chance alone with her was a grueling test in patience.

The opportunity finally came when Lulu fanned a hand over her face at one point, pushed out of her chair and excused herself to get fresh air on the balcony.

“I’ll go with you.” Alwan stood quickly, his eagerness to escape the crowd and grab a moment with her not going unnoticed.

But other than laughing and flinging them knowing looks, their families didn’t stop them.

As soon as it was just the two of them, he jokingly wiped at his brow and sighed. “Whew. Finally some peace and quiet. I thought we’d be in there, taking pictures, forever.”

Lulu rewarded him with a smile. “It wasn’t that bad. You’re exaggerating.”

“I wish I was. Look, it’s already past eight. How did three hours fly by so quickly? Who takes photos for that long even?”

“Stop,” Lulu said, snorting a giggle.

Hearing her laughter soothed his worry that she had been uncomfortable about the party this whole time. Feeling a little better, he still apologized. “Listen, I should’ve checked in with my parents. I honestly never thought they were planning anything like this, and if I’d known, I would've shut it down. I'll understand if you're upset with me."

"You think I'm angry at you?"

He stuffed his hands in his trouser pockets. "Aren't you?"

She shook her head. "I'm not mad. Surprised, yes, but that's kind of the whole point of the party."

"I guess it is," Alwan said with a chuckle.

Lulu smiled back. "Also, even if I was irritated, I still wouldn't have wanted you to say anything to your parents. They might have suspected something."

He nodded slowly, her reasoning clear to him.

"Besides, look at it this way, everyone's happy," she said, nudging her head behind them at the glass walls separating the balcony from the restaurant.

Alwan saw what she meant when he glanced back over his shoulder at their families and friends chatting and laughing inside. Turning his head forward again, he looked out at the reds and golds the setting sun painted the sky, the fading light of day rippling off the calm lake, and the breeze a couple degrees cooler as it swept over his face.

"You're right," he said. "Let's not take this moment from them just yet. I mean, we will have to eventually once we finish up our partnership here." Despite knowing this was always how it would end when he'd first asked Lulu to be his fake fiancée, Alwan hadn't given too much thought to how they'd break up. They had agreed early on to let their families know together that it had been a mutual decision. It would be their last act together before they moved on with their lives apart.

And now that it was on the horizon, it suddenly seemed to be the only thing on his mind.

The end of this.

No more reason for him and Lulu to talk or even see each other. Somehow the thought of that pained him physically. He swallowed with difficulty, his chest suddenly a little tighter and his eyes burning a little more. Telling himself that it was because he'd simply gotten used to her presence in his life, and that he'd only be mourning that loss, Alwan found his conviction swaying when he looked over at Lulu and was, as always, floored by his strong attraction to her.

He looked her over, from her springy curls down to her floral print blouse, long frilly skirt and cute strappy heels, and his breath sawed out and his suit suddenly felt too stuffy. Prying his fingers off the balcony railing, he unbuttoned his suit jacket and was in the middle of loosening his necktie when Lulu spoke up softly.

"We'll let them down as gently as we can. As

long as they see that we're both on the same page with the breakup, your parents will understand and my family will too. I believe they'll just want what's best for us."

Lowering his hands off his tie, feeling no better, Alwan jerked a nod and forced a smile. "Of course. Same page. Right."

He wasn't surprised when her brows knitted together and she frowned. "Are you okay?"

Nodding again, he hooked his arms over the railing and stared ahead, finding it hard to look at her and breathe or think normally. "I'm fine. Just thinking…"

"About?"

Not ready to divulge the strong attachment he had to her, Alwan grasped for an excuse and landed on one. "Just the good news that we've scored two tickets to this star-studded charity gala. My parents go every year and try to get me to join them, but I haven't had a reason to until now."

Until you, he wanted to say, but instead he just stared at her for a beat, his attention lowering to her parted lips, his heart rate picking up.

Blinking, he snapped his gaze from her mouth back to her round eyes.

"What I mean is that it'd be a great place to network and build on referrals."

"I bet it'll be good for your practice." Lulu

tipped her head to the side. "When will the gala be happening?"

"In two weeks, not that you should feel pressured to come with me or anything."

"Alwan, we're a couple."

His breath hitched.

Lulu seemed to have heard it too because she bashfully bowed her head and toyed with the dangling silver charm on her purse. "As in we're a couple for now and we have to present a united front, so I'm going with you." She peeked up at the end, her brown cheeks redder, her glossy lips twitching up.

"I… I'd be grateful for the support, thanks." Compelled by a gravitational pull stronger than him, Alwan drew nearer to her. First one step, then another. An outpouring of feverish warmth flared through his body that had nothing to do with the mid-July heat blanketing the city. He raised his hand, held it hovering near her cheek and vibrated with anxiety the second it took her to give him permission.

It was only a quick little jerk of her head, but it was plenty enough for him.

Electricity tingled out from where his fingers and palm cupped her wondrously soft cheek. Smiling, Alwan wasn't shocked at all by the chemistry sizzling between them. It'd been there from the start. From the very moment he clapped eyes on her again in the thick of the Albertan wilderness. And after the attraction came the affection. This strong urge to be near her all the time, to bask in her attention and…

And what?

He had a suspicion of what he wanted, but he couldn't afford to think on it too long. At least he could take comfort in the knowledge he wasn't unaffected alone.

Lulu's long black lashes fluttered, her warm breath teasing over his thumb when he stroked her bottom lip, her sigh floating up to his ears right before she shut her eyes, swayed forward and tipped her head up to him.

For a moment he had a flash of another time they'd been in a similar position.

Only then he had denied them both at the last second.

The self-restraint he'd shown that first time was nowhere to be had now. Not even the fact that they could clearly be seen from the restaurant registered in his head fully. None of it mattered. *Only her. Always her.*

Reading her invitation loud and clear, Alwan lowered his head tortuously slowly and focused his sights on her all-too-tempting mouth.

He was going to kiss her.

Another inch and their lips would connect.

Almost there…

"Alwan!" Malek appeared and they pulled back from each other quickly. "We're taking more group pictures, so if you guys can stop making googly eyes at each other long enough, we need you in here."

Alwan had never wanted to wring his cousin's neck more than in that moment.

Giving him a death glare, he growled, "We're coming," and Malek took the hint and left.

When he looked back at Lulu, she had her face covering her hands but peeped out at him from between her fingers.

"God. How are we even going to go back in there and look everyone in the eye?" she moaned.

Though embarrassed too, Alwan held out a hand to her, his heart thudding faster when she slipped hers into his. "Easy. We'll do it together."

CHAPTER NINE

"OKAY, VELVET OR silk satin?"

Alwan held up two black bow ties, and from where Lulu sat perched in a highly comfortable armchair inside his luxuriously spacious walk-in closet, she could've sworn they looked the same, except for the subtle glossy sheen on the silk option.

"Is there a big difference?" she asked with squinty eyes before throwing her hands up and sighing in frustration. "I doubt anyone will notice or care."

He grinned and laughed lightly. "I will though, and I don't want to be distracted thinking I made the wrong choice and messed up this opportunity to rub elbows with Toronto's elite tonight. That's why I need your help."

Though he was smiling, Lulu sensed the undercurrent of uneasiness in his voice. He hadn't needed to spell it out that he was nervous about the charity gala and the networking he'd have to be doing all evening. She'd probably feel the same way if her business somewhat hinged on making the right connections with the right people. Sympathetic to his plight, she softly sighed and pointed to the bow tie she preferred.

"The silk, then. It matches the lapels of your dinner jacket."

Alwan's brown eyes sparkled at her, and his handsome smile delighted her probably more than it should.

"Silk satin it is." Turning up the collar of his dress shirt, he strolled over to one of two full-length mirrors at the back of the closet and tied the bow tie in a practiced, fluid motion. Whirling back to her, and sounding nervous again, he asked, "Does it look good?"

Her heart panged for him as she nodded reassuringly.

He's really worried, isn't he?

She bit the inside of her cheek, suddenly buffeted by the need to free him of his doubts. Like all her fluttery feelings around him, it confused her, but it didn't stop her from asking, "Are you nervous?"

"Is it that obvious?" Alwan said with a soft laugh, walking over to the glass-topped dark wood storage unit in the middle of the closet. Pulling open one of the drawers, he plucked out studs and a pair of round silver-and-onyx cuff links, and while he clasped them on his dress shirt, he told her, "I'm trying to think positively, really I am, but my mind keeps conjuring up the worst-case scenarios."

"Such as?" Gripping the chair's tufted armrests, Lulu sat forward when he frowned at her.

"Everyone laughs at me. Nobody wants to work with me. I have to close the doors on the practice." He tightened his lips, his hands curling into fists atop the dresser. "It sounds crazy when I say it aloud. Even so, I can't stop worrying that all of it will come true. That I'll fail at everything I try and disappoint the people around me, the ones I love most." Alwan was looking right at her as he said that last part.

Heat flushed through her, her face warmer from it, her toes wriggling under the voluminous skirt of her evening gown, and her fingers curling into the soft fabric of the armrests.

He's talking about his parents, his family. Not you.

As rational as it was, that thought did nothing to cool her body temperature.

What helped in the end was reminding herself that this moment wasn't about her. *It's about him.* Alwan was crying out for reassurance, even if he wasn't saying it out loud, and she just couldn't turn her back on him.

He needs you now.

Keeping that in mind, Lulu forced a calm into

her voice she wasn't feeling at all and said gently, "That could happen, sure. But what if it doesn't? What if, instead, you make connections tonight that not only help your business but also prove you've chosen the right path?"

"I… I don't know." He looked away, his head bowed, shoulders sagging with the invisible burden he carried.

Her body took control and before she fully understood what she was doing, Lulu was out of her chair, the long skirt of her dress sweeping over the plush carpeting in his closet as she walked to where he stood dejectedly.

Taking a sharp breath, Alwan snapped his head up to her when she touched a hand to his fist, his eyes wide with the same surprise she was feeling.

She didn't know why she'd gone to him, or why she was holding his hand. Only that a pressing need to comfort him had pushed her into action and overridden everything else. But now that her brain had caught up with her limbs, rather than letting go of him Lulu kept her hand right where it was, and all because that need to support him and be by his side still overpowered rational thought.

Still took over her mind and body.

And the only way Lulu could see herself

shaking it off was giving it what it demanded. *Help him.*

So, with her palm over his knuckles, she said, "I told you about my divorce, about my…miscarriage."

Without speaking a word, Alwan interlaced his fingers with hers. He squeezed her hand, offering solace through the contact.

A flood of gratitude pinched at her eyes, but blinking fast, Lulu held the tears at bay.

This wasn't about her. She was trying to help *him.*

"What I didn't tell you was that just before I left, right after I purchased the RV, I saw my ex and the subject of trying to restore our marriage came up. I—I almost considered doing it. Going back. Forgetting about my plans to hit the road. I wavered on what path was best for me," she said, her voice an octave above a whisper but cracking like a whip in the hush of his closet.

Seeing Alwan's eyes go soft with sorrow had her rushing through the rest before she lost the courage to continue.

"In the end I realized I had to move forward. That being nervous, even *scared* doesn't mean that you're making a wrong decision. Sometimes it's usually a sign that it's exactly the path you need to be on right now."

Alwan didn't speak immediately, his fingers

gently squeezing hers, his gaze roving over her face. But then he unexpectedly tugged at her hand and pulled her into an embrace.

Lulu froze and let him hold her while her brain processed what was happening and why her heart was hammering against her ribs and her stomach churned from an explosion of butterflies. She didn't know how long they stood like that, but eventually Alwan drew back, his arms still holding her close to him, his warm eyes shining down over her as if she'd just hung the moon for him.

"Luula, I—I don't know what I'd do without you by my side."

His words and adorable stammer slowly melted her and when he hugged her again, she lifted her arms and wrapped them around his middle and shyly pressed her heated face into his chest. For a moment she let herself exist nowhere else but in the cozy security of his embrace.

She knew she'd have to let go soon.

But that only made her want to cling to him even more.

Cling to this life they'd shared together for the past few months.

Being Alwan's fake fiancée wasn't at all what she'd imagined it would be like. And though this wavering in her heart and mind was exactly what she hadn't wanted happening—what she hadn't *ever* thought would happen, Lulu reminded herself that none of it was true. Her affection and attraction, perhaps. She *did* actually like him. But the rest of it was nothing more than a contract with a fast-approaching deadline.

The reality was Alwan could've had any other woman stand in her place right then. He'd pretty much said it himself. She was his first option because of her divorce and the unlikelihood that she'd want anything more from this charade of theirs.

He picked her solely for the reason that she *wouldn't* desire love from him.

That she wouldn't wish for their relationship to be real.

Deluding herself into thinking she was special would only end in the kind of trouble that had her picking up the pieces of her heart all on her own. *Again.*

Lulu was almost relieved then when a familiar pain radiated from her lower back as it was a reminder that she shouldn't be hugging him.

When she groaned softly, Alwan heard her and pulled back instantly, his hands on her upper arms softly kneading her tense muscles and his gorgeous face gripped with concern for her.

Before he could ask, she unclenched her teeth and said, "I'm all right. Just my time of the month, and nothing a pain reliever can't handle." Moving back from him then, she created much-needed space between them and walked over to where she'd left her chain clutch.

Alwan was her shadow, standing close at hand while she took the medicine from her purse.

"It seems like the pain is pretty awful. Do you always manage it this way?" he asked, now scowling and folding his arms.

Annoyance flared through her, hot and steady. It was a welcome change to the longing ache left behind after she'd pulled away from him. "Yes, not that it's any of your business. Because sometimes that's all that helps. Also, I'm very careful about the amount I take."

"I didn't mean to offend you," he said, sighing after and lowering his arms, hurt blooming over his face.

It was hard to stay angry with him looking at her that way.

Even harder when he explained, "Hashim had a sports injury, a severe one that had him relying on strong pain medication for a long time before we…we lost contact with him. I didn't mean to conflate your pain with my hang-ups on the subject."

If any upset lingered, it was obliterated with his apology. The urge to embrace him once again swept over her, but before it could pull her under, Lulu stumbled back to the large closet's exit with the excuse of needing water. Then she hurried away, sailing out of his bedroom and even considering heading straight for the private elevator to his condo and fleeing his home all together.

But she stopped herself from going that far.

Because I promised him.

And she intended to uphold her end of their deal. That meant the closest thing to sanctuary before they left for the charity gala was a moment of time alone in the kitchen.

Lulu pulled a bottle of chilled water from his fridge and perched herself on one of the stools at the kitchen island. She was looking around absently when she noticed one of the cabinet doors of the built-in pantry was slightly ajar, caught on something. Feeling nosy, she slid off the stool and walked over to pull the door open wider and jumped back when a closed bag of dry cat food landed on the kitchen floor.

She stared down at it, confused as to why Alwan had cat food of all things. As far as she knew he had no pets.

Unless it's for Blueberry...

"There's no way," she murmured with a shake of her head, already reaching down to lift the bag off the floor and place it back where she found it. But just as she set the bag back in the pantry, she startled at the sound of her name and swung around.

Alwan was walking into the kitchen, fully

dressed to the nines now. His eyes landing on her, he stopped at the entrance and tucked his hands in the pockets of his tuxedo pants, his dinner jacket unbuttoned and his dress shirt now paired with a silky waistcoat. He looked beyond good. Like he was ready to conquer the night. *No, the world.*

She smiled, relieved that he seemed to be feeling more confident about the evening, but also pressing a hand to her pounding heart when he slowly moved closer to her.

"Are you feeling better?" he asked, his brow lined with the worry he was tempering from his tone.

Worry for her, she recognized.

Guilt slammed into her. First, for making him concerned about her, but also at the way she'd walked off on him when he'd told her about his brother's plight with pain medication. She only felt worse when she nodded and Alwan smiled, some of the stress easing off his face.

"Are you still angry with me?" he whispered then.

Shaking her head, Lulu bit her lip when the feeling of tears burned at her eyes. It wasn't the first time he'd made her want to cry. And all it did was highlight the fact that despite what she kept telling herself, Alwan had sunken under her skin and burrowed deep into her in a way that she hadn't thought he ever would.

"I *am* sorry if I upset you."

"You didn't," she lied, then sighing, said, "*Fine*, maybe you did a little. But I'm not angry. Not anymore." Certainly not after the way he sweetly apologized and looked genuinely contrite.

His smile a bit wider, Alwan chuckled.

"I'm forgiven, then?"

She tapped her chin, beaming when he laughed a little louder. "I suppose," she said with a put-upon sigh and leaning back against the pantry door she'd forgotten to close. *Oops.*

Alwan was looking there now, but his reaction was unexpected. He glanced away shyly.

Lulu had fully decided to not bring up the cat food, but now that he was acting so strangely about it, she blurted, "Were you planning on getting a cat?"

He avoided her eyes and cleared his throat. "Ah. You found the cat food."

"I did," she said. Then realizing that she was admitting to snooping, hastily added, "I wasn't being nosy. The door was open and I saw it peeking out. I swear."

Alwan tossed her a quick smile. "I believe you. I might have been thinking of looking into local shelters. My home's big but it can get lonely."

That actually made sense. *See. It had nothing to do with Blue or you.* Lulu wasn't sure why she was a little sad about it, but she couldn't pretend that it didn't motivate her when she said, "I could help you, if you want?"

"I'd like that," he replied, not leaving her hanging in suspense.

"Okay, then."

"Okay," he said huskily, only this time his smile had an edge of sexiness, his attention fully on her and her alone. The intensity of his stare had her blushing and walking back to the kitchen island to take a big swig from her water bottle.

Seeming well aware of his effect on her, he dialed up the heat on his seductive smirk before he turned and motioned for her to follow him.

She pointed toward the exit as they headed for his bedroom and walk-in closet again.

"Aren't we leaving?" Lulu asked, and Alwan suddenly spun back to her with that sinful smile and a pair of shoes in each hand.

"Sure. But right after you help me again. So, which will it be? Classic patent leather or crystal-embellished loafers?"

For all the years that Alwan had been dodging his parents' invitations to their parties, he could finally understand what the fuss was all about now that he was at one.

It seemed that all of Toronto's richest and most privileged had stepped out of their opulent homes and off their chartered planes to fete the night in style. And there wasn't a shortage of glitz and glam. From fashionable evening wear to the luxury vehicles the guests were all arriving in, everything oozed wealth in all the splendiferous ways that affluence could be flaunted. Even the venue that the charity gala was being hosted at set the sumptuous tone for the evening.

Situated in one of Toronto's oldest and most luxurious hotels, the ballroom harkened back to a time long past. Tall, vaulted ceilings decorated with oil paintings, gilded pilasters, arched windows and magnificent crystal chandeliers made the expansive ballroom a sight to behold and gave it an air of timelessness.

Like many other guests, Lulu was taking videos and photos with her phone, documenting everything and everyone she met. Alwan couldn't get enough of her glittering eyes winging over to him whenever she glimpsed a celebrity she recognized, and he loved that the noise forced her to lean into him frequently so she could communicate. Her sweet, warm breath teased his ear every single time, her peppery, resinous fragrance imprinting on his lungs, and her long painted nails secured on his arm as they navigated the packed ballroom to their table.

"I don't see your parents yet," Lulu said, her head craning this way and that, her glossy, natural curls even springier than usual and pinned up at her crown. Her beautiful hair bounced with her every step as they searched the ballroom for his mother and father.

Worried he'd lose her in the crowd between the dance floor and the rapidly filling tables, Alwan took hold of her hand and tucked it in the crook of his elbow. "Let's find our table first and then I'll message them."

He wasn't in any hurry to hunt for his parents.

Although he recognized and was grateful that they had helped him get this far with their professional and social connections, he had done plenty of work too. Besides, this was something they couldn't assist him with even if they wanted to. And he had Lulu there for support. Alwan couldn't think of anyone else he'd want by his side right then. He'd even already decided that if nothing else came of the night, at least he was able to share it with her.

It's not like we have a lot of moments like this left.

When that happened soon, in about a month, he'd miss her more than he ever conceived he would or thought possible. Had he known he'd feel this way about her, Alwan would never have proposed the fake engagement to her.

Not that he regretted it.

How could he when looking at her, touching her, breathing the same air as her made him so wholly, incomprehensibly, *deliriously* happy?

Alwan aimed a dopey smile down at her as she looked around and snapped more photos, seemingly oblivious to his powerful feelings for her. Meanwhile he wondered how any of this had transpired. After the lengths he'd gone to avoid it. The sudden trip to Alberta, the fake engagement, even his decision to choose her and not any other woman—none of it had stopped him from doing the very thing he'd planned would never happen to him.

I love her, don't I?

He knew the answer, and so did his heart as it skipped a beat every time Lulu so much as beamed up at him or clutched her fingers tighter around his arm.

I love her, he thought as they reached their table and greeted the other guests already seated.

He should've been happy about the arranged seating because there was a popular reality TV doctor, a pair of brand influencers with tens of millions of followers between them, an A-list actor and even a Grammy-award-winning rapper he often listened to on his commutes to work. Though they were all different, they all had three things Alwan needed for his legal practice: success, money and influence. Mingling with the metropolitan elite had been his goal all along, and here was his chance.

But instead of lauding and reaping his good luck, Alwan could barely focus, his attention diverting every other second to his very lovely—*very fake*—fiancée beside him and the fact that he loved Lulu so fiercely he could think of nothing else.

And he might have wasted the whole night doing just that had Lulu not intervened.

She made it look natural, lightly bumping her foot against his beneath the table, waiting until he looked at her before leaning in, her hand falling over his chest right above his thumping heart, her face drawing near until her lips hovered next to his ear.

"Are you okay?"

He jerked a nod, hyperfocused on every part of her. Her temptingly sweet perfume, her soft brown eyes, her glistening lips and her soft curls brushing his cheek as she moved in closer to whisper in his ear again.

"Just remember, believe in your dream," she said. "It's worth it, all right?"

Not knowing what to say, Alwan grasped her hand atop his chest and squeezed lightly, his thumb caressing the inexpensive but pretty ring she'd bought herself. It should've reminded him that their relationship was built on nothing more than lies they were using to fool the world into believing they were in love. But a yearning for her, *for this* to be real roared in him instead.

Keeping it from showing on his face when she searched his eyes was probably the toughest thing he'd done in a long while, but Alwan knew he succeeded when Lulu smiled beautifully and turned back to strike up a chat with their guests.

He followed her lead and started rubbing shoulders.

By the time the charity event officially kicked off, their hosts introducing themselves and the worthy cause that everybody had gathered to support and donate generously to, Alwan had traded contact details with half of their table and made promising connections with the rest.

The exquisite high-end dinner was worth the thousands his ticket and Lulu's had cost him. After six courses, each more decadent and elaborately plated than the rest, Alwan almost worried he'd pop the studs and buttons off his dress shirt. So when a chamber orchestra started up a lively waltz and other gala attendants moved to the dance floor, he held a hand out to Lulu.

But she shook her head and leaned in to whisper, "I've never danced to this kind of music."

He wasn't having it, and eventually she relented with a sigh, slid her hand in his and Alwan grinned so wide his facial muscles strained from the force. Having her in his arms made the world bleed away until only they existed, just the two of them on the dance floor, swaying and twirling to the music.

For all her doubt, Lulu naturally took to the steps, never once crushing his toes. She glided in his arms, resplendent in her gown. Her crimson dress was so tonally embellished, it glimmered with her movement, every swish of the skirt's hem whispering over the ballroom's highly polished hardwood floor. She'd added a waist-length, matching sequined cape for what he supposed was modesty, but his eyes zeroed in on the tantalizing hints of the dress's thin straps and her warm brown skin through the cape's sheer material.

A fantasy of him teasingly peeling the cape and dress off her flashed through his mind. So vivid was the daydream, Alwan almost stopped them mid-twirl, reached out and plucked open the clasp to the cape at the hollow of her throat.

Instead of falling to his primal urges, he spun her around a few more times, holding her closer to him with each graceful loop around the other dancing couples on the floor. It should've satisfied him to be this near to her. His hand on her back, her warm, soft body pressed to his, her glittering eyes, awed smiles and chiming laughter all directed at him.

All his.

Possessiveness drummed a beat in his head that matched his fast-marching heart rate, and it nearly drowned out the finishing chord of the waltz. At the last moment he dipped her in a flourish, pulling her back up slowly against him until their bodies were flush.

Until Alwan realized that not even that was enough for him.

As the orchestra moved on to a classical pop cover, he pulled down closer to her to be heard over the noise. "Do you want to head out?"

She gave him a nod, allowing him to lead her off the dance floor and back to their table to grab her sparkly clutch purse.

"Won't your parents worry about us?" she asked as they walked through the hotel foyer.

"My mom already texted," he said. "They're having fun with their friends, and knowing them, that means they won't be leaving anytime soon."

"And you're sure you want to leave without saying hello to them?"

He nodded vigorously, not even bothering to hide that he was eager to have Lulu all to himself right now. Nothing short of a fire in the ballroom would make him go back to see his parents and leave her.

Outside, the city's bright lights and loud hum greeted them and he welcomed the mild night breeze on his heated face.

"I'll admit that ballroom dancing was *way* more fun than I'd thought it would ever be," she exclaimed breathlessly, all smiles, her chest heaving from the exertion still.

"It usually gets easier with practice."

"Does it?"

"I'm no professional, and I've spent most my adult life dodging these kinds of events, but I picked up the skill anyway."

Lulu smiled at him before she closed her eyes and tipped her face up to the light breeze, a sigh drifting from her full, glossy red lips. "I can smell the lake from here."

"We're close to the Harbourfront, so that's not surprising. Why don't we take a walk down there?"

They strolled the streets, chatting easily about their jobs, their families and friends, the celebrities at the gala—everything but what his head and heart truly wanted to discuss. In the leisurely twenty-minute walk to the harbor, Alwan waged an internal battle between what he desired and what he'd always believed wasn't meant for him.

He didn't think he could lower his guard long enough to let love creep in.

Yet now that it had, he never wanted it to leave him…

But it had with Hashim, a cynical little voice whispered.

He'd loved his brother so much, and hadn't ever thought that helping him would lead to Hashim leaving him forever. That kind of betrayal left a mark. A wound. A valuable lesson that trusting others only increased his odds of being let down and catching hurt feelings.

With Lulu, the odds of him getting hurt were even higher because their relationship hadn't been meant to last. They had both always known that there was an ending.

That the end was soon.

That they probably wouldn't have a reason to be in each other's lives again after this.

If he kept this up, Alwan was risking a broken heart again.

And yet all of that hadn't put enough fear in him to run away. Hadn't stopped him from touching a hand to her arm and calling out her name when they arrived at the lakefront.

"Luula, wait. As lovely as this all is," he said, sweeping a hand out to the city towering before them on one side and the dark, glittering water of the lake on the other. "Truthfully, there's a reason I wanted us out here, alone."

She laughed, the fluted sound nervous. "Maybe

I've listened to too much true crime, but is this the part where you kill me by drowning me in the lake?"

He smiled and shook his head slowly.

"Then what? Because you look scarily serious."

Alwan unbuttoned his dinner jacket and tucked his hands in his trouser pockets. He then faced the water, finding it easier and faster to organize his helter-skelter thoughts when he wasn't looking at her. "There's something I've been meaning to tell you. Something I've kept from you."

"Okay, *now* you're freaking me out," she said with another anxious laugh.

Hearing the small thread of fear in her voice nearly had him reconsidering all of this. *There's still a chance to walk this back...*

To walk away for good.

As soon as he thought it though, Alwan knew he couldn't do that.

He'd been thinking about this moment with her all night. Waited patiently for it through the gala and obsessed over every detail as he played out the steps he'd take. And now that he had his opportunity, the idea of letting it slip through his fingers didn't sit right with him.

I have to tell her.

But first he nudged his chin out at the obsidian lake to the now-dark islands. "Have you ever been to the Island?"

"No, but I've always wanted to go. Why?"

"No reason except that every time I look at it, I remember my brother. Hashim and I used to go out there all the time, especially during the summers. First with our parents, but then when we were old enough, they'd let us go on the ferry all on our own.

"We'd pretend we were pirates. The ferry our pirate ship and the island the perfect hideaway for all our treasure." Alwan clenched his jaw at the memories flooding back, the good and the bad times with Hashim melding in together.

"Life felt…easier then. Like we were in control of our destinies and nothing could hurt us."

He swallowed, the slow, convulsive pull of his throat giving him all of two seconds to put his brave face on and finish what he'd started. "But that wasn't true. Hashim was hurting quietly for years after his sports injury. His surgery was successful, but the doctors had only healed him on the outside. Inside, he wasn't the same. He was suffering and I… I didn't see it until it was too late.

"I was his brother. I should've known. Should have seen the signs."

"Alwan, I'm so sorry," she said, her soft voice closer than he realized.

"I am too. But that doesn't change anything. Because I let him slip through the cracks and didn't catch him. I failed him. Failed my brother."

Her hand alighted on his arm, her fingers squeezing him until he finally gave in and looked at her.

"You can't think that way. You'll only hurt yourself."

"I can't help it though." His heart twisted in his chest for Hashim and all that his brother was once and had lost to addiction. "This guilt, it's become a part of me."

"Alwan..." She gripped his arm with both hands now, her brows pinched together, lovely mouth downturned and eyes darker, rounder and glimmering with sorrow for him.

He didn't think it could happen, but in that moment, right then and there, it truly felt like Lulu was hurting and grieving almost as much as he was.

When her chin quivered, he cupped her face, smiling down sadly at her. A need to comfort her took hold of him, and not thinking, simply reacting, he leaned into her until his lips settled on her forehead.

She inhaled, tensing a heartbeat before she relaxed, her gentle sigh drifting up to him.

And she sighed again when Alwan wrapped his arms around her, touched his forehead to hers and gazed deeply into her eyes, feeling a serenity he hadn't in a long time.

"I love you."

The words fell from his lips far more easily than he imagined they would.

Though she was quiet after he uttered the confession, he knew she'd heard him because her eyes had gone wide.

"I can't tell you when it happened, and I know it goes completely against what this fake engagement was supposed to be, but…but I can't stop. I've tried. I really have. And apparently, it's not a faucet I can just shut off at will."

When she didn't speak, Alwan began worrying and urged, "Luula, say something…please."

She blinked, whatever shocked trance she was in wearing off, and even before she pushed her hands on his chest, he knew what was coming.

Letting her go, Alwan watched her carve distance between them and dropped his now-leaden arms and reminded himself to breathe through the thorny pain already vining around his throbbing heart. He'd prepared for this. Knew this was always a fifty-fifty possibility. Steeled himself for it happening.

And yet now that it was, now he was looking at her and seeing her guardedness against him, he realized he could've never protected himself from this.

Stupid, he thought. What had he been thinking? That the scenery alone would sway her mind when she'd made it *very* clear to him and *very* early on that she didn't want a relationship again?

Did he really think she would make an exception for him?

I'm so stupid.

Alwan gritted his teeth and clenched and unclenched his fists, his fingers still burning with the memory of holding her a minute ago.

She still hadn't said a word. Hadn't even acknowledged his love for her.

He shook his head, but it did nothing to dislodge the hurt and humiliation now taking hold of him. The longer he stood out there, the more the reality of his rejection sank in, and the sharper the heartache became. "Let's head back," he said, hating the brusque tone he used but knowing that the anger masked the anguish quickly consuming him.

Arms now wrapped around herself, eyes ever-wide and alert and full of wariness, Lulu nodded silently.

It struck him that the walk back to the hotel was markedly different in tone this time around. Where before they were conversing contentedly about anything and everything, now the atmosphere between them was thickly oppressive with all that they'd left unsaid.

When they arrived back at the upscale historic hotel, Lulu finally ended her silence.

"I'm going to grab a cab." She was already walking in the direction of the taxi stand outside the hotel.

Her declaration caught him by surprise. They'd arrived together, so he had just assumed that she would catch a ride back with him.

Why would she want to be near you after everything that just happened?

Jaw clenched, Alwan stepped toward her, his offer to drive her home on the tip of his tongue.

But at the last moment he stopped himself. If this was what she desired—if she truly wanted the space apart from him, then he'd respect her wishes. Still, it took all his strength to remain on the curb while Lulu gathered the long skirt of her gorgeous dress and slid into the back of a taxi. He didn't breathe until the car drove away. Didn't turn his back and leave until the cab ferrying her from him had melded with downtown traffic.

Now, if only he could turn and walk away from this still-beating love he had for her.

CHAPTER TEN

Two weeks.

That was the first thought in Alwan's mind when he woke up to the bluish-gray light of dawn glowing through his bedroom windows.

It'd been a full fourteen days since that fateful night he confessed his love to Lulu. Two of the longest weeks of his life, not only because he hadn't seen, called or texted her and had taken her silence as a sign to give her all the space she needed, but also because he'd been debating on what it meant for their fake engagement.

Since they'd pushed their deadline up to Labour Day, they had a few weeks left on the clock.

Technically he could hold her to that date. But it hadn't felt right using it to force his company on her. Though if he was being honest, he'd considered the underhanded tactic. *If only to see her...*

In the end the better part of him had won out and Alwan had nixed the idea of manipulating her into spending time with him. He even told himself that the distance and time apart would lessen this hungering ache and persistent longing for her.

But he should've known that time didn't really heal wounds.

If it had that power, would he still feel shame and remorse every time he thought of Hashim?

More and more now, he'd been thinking of his runaway brother. He knew it was partly because of Lulu and her rejection, but the other part was finally understanding that a lot of his decisions of late had been influenced by what had happened in the end with Hashim.

Without realizing it, Alwan had allowed his choice to answer his brother's call and get him away from the addiction treatment center to shape much of his life. From feeling guilty for hiding his role in Hashim's escape from their parents, to feeling like he'd owed them happiness and giving in to their desire to see him married. All of which then led him to seeking out Lulu and proposing the fake engagement in the first place. Before finally, culminating in him falling hard for her, telling her that he loved her—

And getting my heart broken.

Really, it was all his fault. He couldn't do anything about Hashim anymore, not when he didn't even know if his brother was alive or long gone from this world. But he could help Lulu by ending this now.

It would go against their agreement to announce their breakup mutually and together, but he couldn't ask her to do that after he'd dumped his feelings on her. No, he'd shoulder the blame all on his own. By the time she learned what he had done, the truth will have already come out.

Anyway, it's not like I haven't broken any of our rules.

He'd touched and hugged her. Kissed her—albeit only on the forehead, yet still.

More than the physical intimacy they had promised to avoid was the emotional connection they'd made. At least on his part, it had felt like she'd opened up to him and let him get near to her vulnerabilities. And he'd done the same, even coming close to sharing his secret about how it'd been his fault that Hashim had run off and disappeared. He had confided in her. *Trusted* her.

Loved her.

It hadn't been enough to change her stance on relationships though.

As he showered, dressed and left his place to drive over to his parents' home, Alwan ruminated on that and hoped that she'd see ending their fake engagement as the olive branch it was. *Maybe this doesn't have to be the end...*

It was that small silver lining he'd clung to as he rang the doorbell and greeted his parents' housekeeper at the front door of the Tudor-style mansion.

Alwan found his mother and father in the drawing room, the gleaming cherry oak walls and coffered ceiling warmed by vintage-inspired brass wall sconces. His father sat in the lone armchair across the white marble fireplace, a double-wall glass mug full of tea in one hand and a newspaper in the other, his readers perched at the edge of his long, thick nose as usual. His mother sat on the sofa and leaned over the coffee table, peering through a photo album while stacks more were littered on the sofa cushions on either side of her.

They both looked up when he entered.

"Salaam Yumma, Abu," he said, squeezing his father's shoulder as he passed behind him and then bending down so his mother could kiss him on the cheek.

She made room for him on the sofa before giving him a curious look. "Although I love when you drop in unannounced, habibi, it also worries me. Is there anything wrong?"

His father lowered the paper he was reading, his bushy graying brows hiked up with intrigue.

Alwan gulped, realizing right then that his intention to tell them the truth might not be as simple as he thought.

"Alwan?" his mother called to him, her hand

squeezing his leg, the gesture meant to be comforting but only heightening his guilt.

Choosing cowardice, he said, “No, nothing’s wrong. I… I just wanted to see you both, that’s all.”

“Isn’t that sweet?” his mother gushed, pinching his cheek. “How did we get to be such lucky parents?”

Alwan’s father snorted lightly and was already lifting his paper up, but not before Alwan caught his warm smile.

Their praise swelled his chest with joy, momentarily numbing his guilt at the secrets he kept from them.

Wanting to hold on to the happiness a little longer, Alwan pointed to the photo album open on the glass coffee table. “What are you doing? Rearranging photos?” She had some of the pictures pulled out of the plastic pockets and spread out on the coffee table around a gold tray holding a tea set.

“I was, but then I became distracted,” his mother said, nodding as she poured him a cup of shai.

“I haven’t looked at some of these albums in so long. I almost forgot we took some of these pictures,” she told him once she handed him a teacup.

Picking up one of the albums, Alwan flipped

through a few pages and immediately understood what she felt as memories he'd forgotten came flooding back. He smiled and laughed at most of them, reliving the experiences in those frozen stills of his family's past. Although he should've known it was coming, it still gave him pause when he turned another page in the album and saw a younger Hashim staring back up at him.

In the photo he posed in his rugby jersey, the biggest grin on his face.

"He loved playing so much," his mother reminisced, surprising Alwan because his parents often didn't speak about Hashim.

And she continued to comment as Alwan looked through more of the album, smiling and sighing and even stroking some of the photos as if she could touch Hashim through them. Remorse constricted his chest, the chains tightening when his mother reached for a tissue and wiped her eyes at one point.

"Yumma," he quietly said, contrition squeezing his vocal cords.

"It's fine," his mother insisted with a sniffle. He might have believed her if her lips weren't trembling with the tears she was holding back.

His father lowered his newspaper swiftly and set his mug on the coffee table. "Stop looking at those if they're making you so sad. Put them away, Alwan. Put all of them away," he said firmly, his scowl fearsome.

Shaking her head, his mother pulled the album away from Alwan gently before he could even consider following his father's stern instruction.

"There's no reason to do that. He's still our son after all."

His father huffed and flung his hands out. "Son? What son abandons his parents and his younger brother?"

Alwan winced, not so much at his father's raised voice but the angry hurt in his tone as he hurled the words.

"Hashim is *our* son. No matter what happened, nothing will ever change that for me," his mother said, a fire in her teary eyes as she clutched the album to her chest, hugging the only connection to her other son that remained.

"Do what you want, but all of this—" his father stabbed his finger at the albums on the coffee table and the sofa "—all it does is bring us pain that I want no part of."

His mother covered her face with her hands and his father's pale brown cheeks were so red that Alwan worried he'd pop a vein.

"It's my fault," he whispered, the silence in the room amplifying his quiet voice and making his words crash as loud as thunder.

Both his mother and father snapped their heads to him.

Closer to him, his mother set the album aside and took his hands in her own. But Alwan pulled his hands away from her, unable to take her comfort without his culpability choking him completely. And before that happened, he needed to tell them everything—

All of it.

"I'm the one that you should blame. Not each other," he said.

"Alwan," his mother said, reaching for his hands again and holding on tighter this time, "your abu and I don't blame each other. And we would never blame you. What happened with Hashim, his sickness, it was not his fault either."

Alwan shook his head slowly, his eyes downcast and filling up. "It *is* my fault though. I'm the reason that Hashim is gone. I am why he isn't here with all of us now. I… I helped him escape. It was me. He called me and he asked if I could come to get him. I understand now why he had to go to the treatment center, but back then all I thought was that he needed me and I had to help him."

He then told them how he took the car, drove with only his learner's permit to the treatment center and picked his brother up after Hashim had snuck out of the building.

All these years and it just came pouring out of him, the dam completely broken, his vision swimming as he blinked free the first of his tears. At the end, having run completely dry of words, Alwan squeezed his eyes shut and covered them with a hand, crying quietly.

His mother embraced him, her warm bakhoor fragrance taking him back to all the times he'd skinned his knees and needed her comfort to ease the pain. Only this pain was burrowed so much deeper and had lived with him for so much longer.

Pulling him back by the shoulders eventually, his mother cupped his chin and forced him to look her in the eye.

"Alwan, we know," she said with a tender smile.

Shock swept away his shame and he stared wide-eyed back at her.

She lowered her hand from his chin and squeezed his shoulders. "We've always known, ya habibi."

Alwan looked between them, his father now sighing and resting back in his armchair.

"How?" he breathed.

"The treatment center caught you both on their security cameras. They told us the same night they reported that Hashim had left."

Alwan couldn't believe his ears. All this time

he'd been hiding what he thought was some big, dark secret—all these years of worrying that he'd hurt them, and all he'd been doing was torturing himself. "W-why didn't you tell me?"

His mother gave him a pained look and patted his hands now. "We thought that it was for the best. That if we said anything, you'd blame and never forgive yourself. But it seems we inflicted the very harm we were trying to avoid." She hugged him again, squeezing him so tightly his ribs hurt but in a good way. "We're sorry, habibi. We should have said something from the beginning."

Alwan nodded and held still as his mother kissed him on the cheeks.

"Your yumma is right, Alwan," his father said, his expression softer now. "Put it out of your mind that it's your fault. It's no one's fault. Your brother simply made his decision to move on without us. If he ever chooses to return, then we'll welcome him. He is after all our son."

His mother beamed and squeezed Alwan's hands. "Now do you feel better?"

"I do," he said with a small smile. He did feel better without the weight of his secret about Hashim, but he was instantly reminded of the real reason he'd come over when his mother gave him a long look.

"And was that why you came over, or is something else bothering you? Because I had another reason for looking at these photo albums. I was seeing if there was room for more pictures once you and Luula get married."

Hearing Lulu's name had him tensing all over once more.

Especially when his mother said, "I haven't seen her in a while."

He opened his mouth, fully prepared to divulge his other secret. But before he could tell his parents that his and Lulu's engagement was a fabrication, his mother frowned at him.

"Alwan, have you done something to upset her again? Because if you have, I already told you that apologizing and communicating are very important to marriage."

If he knew that a simple apology would fix everything, Alwan would've already been down on his knees in front of Lulu a long while ago.

"She's just busy," he lied.

His mother didn't look like she believed him, but she slowly nodded. "Very well. But you bring her along with you next time, and tell her that we miss her."

I miss her too.

Two weeks without seeing and hearing from her was breaking him. After he left his parents, he sat in his car in their long, cobbled driveway and replayed that last night with her. Only now he realized that he hadn't given her a chance to talk. She'd been silent, yes, but he had jumped to the conclusion that she was rejecting him.

And maybe she wasn't, he thought, hope budding in him.

Maybe it'd be like with his parents, when he'd been so certain that they'd resent him for the role he'd played in Hashim's disappearance and the exact opposite was true.

Sitting up straighter, Alwan started his engine and sped off onto the busy city streets, already mapping out a game plan on how he'd try and shoot his shot with Lulu again.

And it either worked this time…

Or I let her go forever.

"Should I text him?" Lulu asked Blue, brushing a comb down his back in smooth, gentle strokes. They were sitting in the middle of her bedroom, her legs crossed and Blue dozing off in front of her. He opened his eyes and gave her a big yawn.

She sighed. "You're right. It's probably a bad idea." But even as she said it, Lulu's mind wandered over to Alwan, just as it had every day for the past two weeks. Not only had he become her waking thought, his face was the last thing she saw when she drifted off to sleep every night. And she wasn't even counting the dreams she'd been having of him lately. Dreams she wished she could say were pleasant, but were mostly variants of the same event: the night he confessed to her.

If that wasn't enough, Lulu had replayed that evening over and over in her head since then and still cringed at her reaction every single time.

When Alwan had told her he loved her, she'd just *frozen* up. There was no other way to describe it except that she had become a human statue. She didn't think she'd ever been that mortified in her life. Especially when Alwan asked her to say something and all she could do was stare at him like a deer trapped in headlights.

It's not like it's my fault. He surprised me.

She hadn't expected him to tell her that he loved her.

Sure, there had been the confusing electrical undercurrents of *something* that felt a lot like unbridled attraction and desire between them. But lust wasn't *love*. It wasn't the passion she heard in his voice as he'd said those three words to her, the reverence in his dark eyes as he looked at her, and it most definitely wasn't the heartbreak on his face when she hadn't given him a response.

Not even the barest reaction. No wonder he hasn't even messaged...

Lulu bit her lip, her frustration at the situation tangling up with her guilt. She was so caught up in her emotions, her brushstrokes snagged over

Blue's fluffy white coat. No longer relaxed, he yowled at her immediately, batting his pink toe beans at the comb before bounding up onto all fours and prowling away from her, his tail raised indignantly.

"Sorry," she murmured after him, setting the comb aside and drawing her knees up to her chest.

She wasn't in the best control of her emotions as of late. It felt as if Alwan's confession had flung open the doors on the long-sealed part of her that had sworn off of romantic relationships and love in general. Because of him, now—after all this time—he had her wondering "what if?"

What if Lulu told him that she reciprocated his attraction?

What if she had said that these past few months faking an engagement with him had been the most thrilling of her life?

But most of all, she wondered what if she had said and done anything but the *nothing* she'd ended up doing.

Lulu's gaze drifted to her bed, knowing that the suitcase underneath was a good part of the reason she had gone silent when Alwan had told her that he loved her. Before she knew it, she had moved there and pulled it back out.

Smoothing her hands over the hard shell, she

remembered why she'd held on to the suitcase all this time.

First it was a symbol of her loss, but then it had become a reminder of why love was dangerous and why she shouldn't give herself the hope of ever trying for a family again.

But now, when Lulu looked at it, it just felt like it no longer belonged.

Picking up her phone, she pulled up to sit on the edge of the bed and rubbed between Blue's ears as she scrolled through to find the locations of the nearest donation bins. "I'm ready to let go," she told him when he nuzzled her hand with his face, his wet nose and rough tongue scraping over her fingers. The peace she felt was inexplicable…and also short-lived as a text from Alwan pinged in her inbox.

Need to talk. Will you meet me here?

He sent a location pin, and Lulu was intrigued to see it was Ward's Island, one of the Toronto Islands.

She already knew her response even before she sent it, but her excitement to see him melded with a trepidation over what he might have to say to her and how she'd react this time.

Figuring she could use a companion, Lulu peered down at Blue and asked, "Want to go on an adventure?"

* * *

Getting off the ferry, Lulu messaged Alwan and wasn't kept in suspense for long.

He texted her back with a live location, and she followed it all the way to him.

"You came," he said, standing in a break between trees at the sandy edge of the island. He looked nervous as he swiped his hands over his thighs and strolled up to her, wearing another of his handsome business suits. "I thought you might not, given how we left things last."

She wasn't surprised he'd said that. Just as Alwan hadn't believed she would show up, Lulu hadn't expected for him to text her, let alone with an invitation to meet up. Honestly, she wouldn't have been shocked if he'd just ended the fake engagement and moved on. The fact he hadn't and that he appeared happy to see her uplifted her mood and gave her some hope that, maybe, this wasn't the end after all…

From inside his carrier, Blue meowed loudly and insistently until she let him out and strapped him in his harness and leash.

Alwan chuckled softly.

"I should've known you two would come as a package," he rumbled above her, shocking her when he crouched down next to her. Though she didn't mind him being so close, Blueberry bared his fangs and hissed at him. "After all this time, he still doesn't like me. Is it because I didn't invite him?"

Stifling a grin at the adorable pout on Alwan's face, Lulu played along and shrugged. "Who knows? Maybe."

"Okay, fine, my ego's taken a hit. But one of these days, I'll win him over," he vowed, smirking at her.

It was the conviction in that promise that had her heart juddering faster. Because it sounded awfully like he was planning to see her cat again.

Which means he's planning to see me.

Hope washed through her as Alwan slowly rose up to full height and offered his hand to her. Grasping it gently, Lulu blushed when his fingers squeezed hers and lingered after he'd helped her up.

When he did eventually let her go, he rubbed at his bearded jaw, the edginess she'd felt from him earlier rushing back.

"First, before I say anything, I want to apologize for my behavior on our last night together," he said with a frown, his brow lined with tension. "I… I should have been more understanding to you after I'd said what I said."

After he'd told her that he loved her, he meant.

The pressure over Lulu's chest pressed down harder, her guilt intertwining with the same pining she'd endured the last two weeks being apart from him. She opened her mouth to tell him that it wasn't his fault. That he'd shocked her with his confession, and that she'd been so confused, so unable to accept that he could care for her.

That he could love me.

But before she could utter a word, Alwan moved on.

"I should have let you understand what I was feeling and why. So, I'm going to fix my mistake and do that now. Starting with telling you the truth of what happened with my brother… and me. Because Hashim didn't just run away on his own. I helped him."

Lulu listened as Alwan told her about how his older brother had called him up and asked for a ride to leave the treatment center he was admitted to for his addiction. How after Alwan had shown up, Hashim had asked to be dropped off at the nearest train station.

"I didn't know that he'd buy a ticket to the next departing train and never look back. I sat there waiting in the car for almost an hour before I realized that he wasn't coming back, realized what he'd done and how he'd used me. I couldn't bring myself to tell my parents about the part I'd played once they found out that Hashim had left.

"I held on to that secret so long that I'd convinced myself they'd hate me if I ever revealed the truth, when all along my mom and dad knew what I'd done, and had chosen not to ask me about it as a way of protecting me. They worried that if they addressed it I would carry guilt and feel blame, not knowing that I did anyway."

Alwan sighed heavily. "What I'm trying to say is that I've only just realized in the last few days that I allowed what happened with Hashim to run my life. I convinced myself that I couldn't trust anyone, and that I was better off being on my own. And it worked…until you. Being with you these last four months has opened my eyes to just how lonely my life's become.

"Sure, I've got my career aspirations, but they aren't enough."

Lulu's breaths came out shallow, sawing through her lungs as he stepped in closer to her and lifted his hands, his fingers hovering by her cheeks.

"Being with you has made me want something I thought I'd never want. But I also know what you've been through, so after all this, I'll only say this one more time and respect your decision, whatever you choose." He paused meaningfully for a moment before he stopped her world again.

"Lulu, I love you."

Gazing into his eyes, she could see his yearning, adoration and the love he spoke of shining through clearly. Hear it catching deeply in his voice. It should've been enough to cast all her doubts away, but she still held on to one that kept her defensive. Clung to it like a lifeline as a little voice warned that they'd both end up being hurt if this continued.

"Why would you want to be with me?" she asked so softly she barely heard herself. Shaking her head numbly, she said, "I have nothing to offer you. Not the kind of money or prestige you might want in a wife, not even the ability to… to give you a *family.* I'm sure something's long broken inside of me."

"Lulu—"

"It's true," she said, speaking over him, her eyes filling with tears. "I don't know if I could love again, and I don't know if I'm ready to risk being hurt by someone I care for deeply. Do you know what it feels like to watch someone you love look at you like a stranger? See their love for you eroding before your eyes?" She blinked and freed her tears, let them track down her cheeks as she tipped her head back to look at Alwan head-on. "I'm *broken.*"

He framed her face with his hands, his gaze boring into her, his expression stern. "I don't believe that."

"You should," she whimpered. "Have I told you why I called my cat Blueberry? And, no, it's not because of his eye color.

"I got him the same week I found out I was

pregnant. Seven weeks pregnant. My baby was just about the size of a blueberry…" Lulu let out a humorless laugh. "That's why you shouldn't want this. Want me. I can't give you what you want."

"What I want," Alwan began, lowering his head and leveling their eyes, "is right here."

"You don't mean that," she whispered.

"I do though," he argued gently.

"Well, what if you want a family? I'm sure your parents or mine want grandkids to spoil rotten someday and if I can't…"

"Then we don't," he said.

"Okay, but what if I decide I want to leave the city and travel some more?"

"Well, then I'd be willing to try a long-distance relationship."

"But—" She broke off with a muffled moan as Alwan kissed her for the first time, his lips coaxing hers to respond, the heat between them as electric and consuming as she'd always known it would be. When he broke off, he stayed close to her, their noses touching, hot breaths mingling, and his love staring back at her, his arms now holding, comforting and reassuring her.

"Are you sure?" she asked, breathless and still floating from his kiss.

Alwan's laugh melted her lingering doubt and stopped her tears.

"I'm certain that I love you, Lulu, and no matter how you think I feel or *should* feel, it doesn't change that fact. Doesn't change that I long for you. I. Love. You." He punctuated his declaration with little soft kisses to her parted lips.

"And you're sure you won't resent me later?"

"Resenting you would be like resenting myself, and I could never do that to me, and most definitely not to you." Then Alwan kissed her again, and Lulu felt it through her body, in her buzzing heart and head and right down to her soul.

"I can see why you like this place so much," Lulu said, looking from their tangled fingers and over her shoulder to him. She was sitting between his legs, her back pressed to his front, and her curly hair tickling his face. It was the only place Alwan wanted to be right then.

And forever, he thought happily.

He smiled at her. "It takes ahold of you, doesn't it?"

They looked out at the view of Toronto's skyline, the sun beginning to descend and lighting up the sky and the city in its wash of orange-golden light.

"Beautiful," Lulu said a little while later when the sun glowed behind the CN Tower, the fading light of day glittering in the lake.

Alwan saw exactly what she meant, but he found his stare tracking down to her at one point as he agreed, "Yeah, beautiful." He hugged her, wondering how he'd gotten so lucky.

She must have been thinking the same thing because she said, "I can't believe that a fake engagement did this." Lulu raised their clasped hands and shook her head in awe. "We only broke all our stipulations to get here."

He laughed and pressed a kiss to the heated tip of her ear. "Our little save-the-date charade turned out to be a big hit for us, so I can't complain if some rules were broken along the way."

"Incorrigible," she muttered, but her bright smile told him everything.

"I am, but you love it." He kissed her cheek, delighted when she turned her head to him and presented her soft, luscious mouth. They were both breathless by the time he lifted his head and panted, "Speaking of our charade, what ever happened to your RV repairs?"

"They're actually ready." Lulu looked away, confusing him by her sudden shyness until she explained, "They have been for a week now."

"A week? Why didn't you say so?"

"Because I kind of forgot to check my email with the update. I got so caught up in everything that was happening with us, that it escaped my mind."

Alwan grinned, understanding what she meant exactly. These last two weeks without her had stalled his life almost completely. He hadn't been able to focus on his practice or any work, for that matter. Though he imagined that would change now that Lulu had accepted his love.

"Did you want company to go pick up your motor home?" he asked, toying with the fake engagement ring she'd bought herself. "Alberta's a long way from here."

"I guess you can come. If you don't mind Blueberry coming along too?"

Alwan glanced over to where her cat lounged nearby on a Muskoka chair. "How could I mind it when he's so much a part of you?"

Lulu trapped his chin in her soft hand and slowly pulled up to touch her lips to his, whispering, "I think that's the sweetest thing you've ever said."

"Sweeter than telling you that I love you a whole lot?"

She scrunched her nose adorably. "Okay, maybe that *is* sweeter."

He chuckled and kissed her again, only this time longer and deeper, until her taste filled him, body and soul.

But they were both wrong, because there was something sweeter than their kisses.

"I love you," Lulu said when they took a break to catch their breaths.

It struck him that she hadn't spoken the words

yet, but now that she had, Alwan couldn't believe it. And he asked her to say it again.

"I love you," she repeated with a bashful little smile.

"Say it again."

"I love you."

"Again," he breathed against her mouth, his heart leaping with joy.

And when she whispered, "I love you, Alwan," and kissed him, it left no doubt in his mind that she truly did.

EPILOGUE

"We really did it, didn't we?" Lulu touched the diamond platinum band on her finger, awe at its beauty filling her every time. The halo diamond ring was almost a perfect replica of the fake engagement ring she'd bought herself. Only these diamonds were very real and vividly bright in the hushed, cool darkness of Alwan's latest flashy car, an English white Rolls-Royce. She looked up at him as he took her hand and raised it to his lips, his mouth brushing the ring he'd given her, a symbol of their steady, eternal love.

"We did," he said, his slow, sinful smile stirring up those all-too-familiar butterflies in her stomach. "And now you're mine *for real.*"

"Ditto." She gasped when his hand slid to her wrist and he gently tugged her across the back seat to him. Holding her to his chest, he kissed her with the hunger of a man that had kept his desires in check while they performed the nikah at the masjid.

Sure enough, he nipped her lip and pulled

back, grinning wolfishly at her as he said, "I've been thinking of doing that all through the ceremony, and I might have if I wasn't positive that I'd have scandalized the imam and our families."

Lulu laughed when he smacked another kiss on her.

He cuddled her to him then, his hands wandering to the satin lacing of her corset bodice. She reached around and caught his wrists. "Not here," she whispered, flinging a look at the opaque privacy glass.

"Don't worry. The driver can't see us…or hear us, for that matter," he reassured her when she looked back at him.

"Hear us?" she echoed, confused.

At least she was until Alwan started tickling her, his hands running along her sides, finding all her secret sensitive spots. She wriggled against him, peals of laughter filling the back of the car. Soon her giggled pleas for mercy turned to soft moans when he kissed and nipped along her jawline to her collar and right above her heaving breasts.

She was so caught up in him that she hadn't noticed they had arrived at the venue.

It was Alwan who sat her up and helped smooth her dress of any evidence of their passion. Righting his tux next, he opened the car door, exited and guided her out with a hand before offering his arm to her.

As they walked up to the familiar castle-like mansion together, Lulu beamed up at Alwan, thrilled that he had surprised her by reserving their reception at the Casa Loma. She had fallen in love with the garden grounds and the darkly romantic, majestic stone building. They were supposed to meet their families and friends in the garden, at the glass pavilion she and Alwan had visited once before, but instead of heading down the path she knew would take them there, he steered her toward the parking lot.

"Where are we going?"

He grinned mischievously. "We're almost there, so why spoil the surprise?"

And he was right. After a short walk, Lulu saw what he was alluding to. Her motor home was there rather than where she'd parked it last.

"What's going on?" she asked warily, but still letting him lead her closer to the back of the RV to reveal the surprise.

Lulu covered her mouth with a hand when she saw it.

In big bold dark blue lettering was one word: *Blueberry.*

"Your RV needed a name, and this one felt appropriate." Alwan came up behind her, his arms circling her, his lips near her ear. "If you want to change it though, that's cool too."

Lulu blinked rapidly and sniffled, fanning at her face and crying out, "Alwan, really? My makeup doesn't need this right before our wedding reception." She turned around and hugged him, looking up only when she was sure she wasn't going to tear up. "I can't believe it's been a whole two years. That we started here," she said with a look back at the RV.

In those two years, a lot had happened. After they confessed their love to each other, they'd announced to their families that they wanted to take a step back and explore their relationship. Everyone had been more than happy to support them. And while they dated and got to know each other, Alwan's private practice went on to thrive, and Lulu had chosen to stay in the city with her family and had finally told them about her miscarriage. She and Alwan had even discussed their feelings and hopes about possibly one day having children, and he'd told her that he was happy trying for a family with her only if she wished for it.

Feeling a swell of appreciation and love for him, she sprang up on her toes and pecked his lips.

He stole his own kisses.

"My makeup," she reminded him as he kissed her cheeks and forehead.

Laughing, he took her hand and pulled her into the RV. Locking the door, he turned on her and swept her up into his arms and carried her to the bedroom, right past their two astonished cats. Blueberry and their latest addition Pea, a tiny, big-eared Cornish Rex who Alwan had adopted over a year ago.

"We're going to be late for the reception," she warned.

He shrugged and winked at her. "I'm okay with that. Besides, better late than not showing up."

"Alwan, don't you dare—" Lulu cut off with a squeal as he dropped her onto the bed.

He followed her, covering her body with his and making her forget her protests with his drugging kisses and rapturous caresses. At the end of it, her makeup wasn't the only thing she had to worry about.

As she lay in his arms, both their outfits rumpled, Lulu didn't think he could make her happier.

But then Alwan said, "I took three weeks off and I thought we could travel in the RV for our honeymoon."

She snapped up and looked down at him. "Do you mean it? What about your business? You can't close the office down for three weeks..."

"And I'm not going to. I trust my staff, and I've let my clients know that I'll be spending quality time with my once fake fiancée, now new wife."

"You did *not* tell them about our fake engagement," she griped, swatting his chest.

Alwan caught her hand and pulled her down to him, his thumb stroking over her engagement ring. "I didn't, but it wouldn't have mattered if I had because this is real now and will be always."

"I love you," she said, her heart never so full.

"I love you more."

Lulu rolled her eyes at his ever-present ego, but this time she let it go because his confidence proved that their love was as bright and hopeful as their future together.

* * * * *

If you enjoyed this story, check out these other great reads from Hana Sheik

Another Shot at Forever
Falling for Her Forbidden Bodyguard
The Baby Swap that Bound Them
Forbidden Kisses with Her Millionaire Boss

All available now!